For the *Love* of PETE

A Story of Faith, Family, and Football

A NOVEL

P. Grant Gartrell

ISBN 979-8-88616-424-4 (paperback)
ISBN 979-8-88616-425-1 (digital)

Christian Faith Publishing
832 Park Avenue
Meadville, PA 16335
www.christianfaithpublishing.com

Printed in the United States of America

This book is dedicated to two men who have had a major impact on my life and my walk with the Lord. I thank God for sending these men into my life.

Pastor Dan Hearn, who gave up his time with his family to accommodate my work schedule. For several weeks, we would meet as he led me through the steps of the journey to salvation. Because of his passion to lead others to the Lord, I was adopted into the family of God.

Ray Souders, a true brother in Christ who has been a mentor to me for more than thirty years. He is a gifted teacher who leads our men's weekly Bible study. He has a unique ability to dig deep into the lessons of the Bible. It is through these studies and the example set by him that have kept me on the right path in my walk with the Lord.

To these dedicated servants of God, I am eternally grateful.

CONTENTS

Prologue vii

Chapter 1: The High School Quarterback 1

Chapter 2: Life-Changing News 3

Chapter 3: Brother to Brother 7

Chapter 4: The Call and Meeting 9

Chapter 5: Breaking the News 15

Chapter 6: A Good Problem 20

Chapter 7: Season Wrap-Up 24

Chapter 8: Pete Informs the Family..25

Chapter 9: Preseason Practice 30

Chapter 10: The Season Begins...35

Chapter 11: Preparing for Next Season 39

Chapter 12: Jordan Visits the Farm 42

Chapter 13: The 2007 Season 47

Chapter 14: The Championship Game 52

Chapter 15: Pete's Final Days 57

Chapter 16: Decision Time for Jordan 65

Chapter 17: The Coach's Conversion 68

Chapter 18: The 2008 Season 73

Chapter 19: The Off-Season 75

Chapter 20: The 2009 Season 78

Chapter 21: Decision Time for Trace 81

Chapter 22: God's Plan for All 84

Epilogue 87

PROLOGUE

Early August 2005

The Myers family own and operate a dairy farm in Frederick County, Maryland. The city of Frederick is now Maryland's second largest city; however, there is still a large portion of the county that is rural and a thriving agricultural community.

Peter (Pete) Myers is a second-generation dairy farmer, a devout Christian man who is widely respected in the community. He has always been active in 4-H and FFA (Future Farmers of America) and the Dairyman's Association. He has a passion for teaching farming to young people. He has served as an elder for his church and as a Sunday school teacher for young adults. He and his wife, Judith, have been married for twenty-seven years and have raised four children on the family farm. His favorite saying is, "It's all part of God's plan."

Judith (Judy) Myers, Pete's wife, is a farmer's wife through and through. She and Pete met in their senior year of high school at a Youth for Christ gathering. She had also grown up on a farm. Pete and Judy had so much in common. They married when both of them were twenty years old. She is also active in the community and the church. She has taught Sunday school for elementary age children for many years. Although she prides herself as a homemaker, she is never hesitant to pitch in with the farm work when she is needed.

Brian Myers (age twenty-four) is the oldest son. Following high school, Brian attended the University of Maryland (College of Agriculture). He is now running the dairy operation of the farm. He plans to marry in March of next year.

Dennis Myers (age twenty-two) attended Frederick Community College. After receiving his associate's degree in criminal justice, he enlisted in the US Marine Corps. He is currently stationed at Camp Lejeune, North Carolina.

Lori Myers (age nineteen) is attending Frostburg State University in Western Maryland. She is studying to be a teacher for special needs children. At a very early age, she developed a passion to help disadvantaged children. She comes home from school every weekend and serves as a youth group leader at church.

Trace Myers (age seventeen) is preparing for his senior year at Governor Thomas Johnson High School. The quarterback has led his team to two consecutive state titles. Between his sophomore and junior years, he grew nearly three inches and now stands at six feet, five inches. Despite his weight (228 pounds) and his height, he is a very mobile quarterback. He is currently among the most heavily recruited quarterbacks in the nation. What makes him unique is the fact that he is *ambidextrous.* He is able to throw with either arm with equal strength and accuracy. This allows him to roll out in either direction, making him an even greater threat to opposing defenses and more valuable to any team. He is a natural-born leader but very humble. When asked about his talents, he always replies, "The Lord has blessed me in so many ways." Academically, he is in the top 10 percent of his class.

After being recruited by virtually every major college program in the country, he has not yet made a commitment. Over this past summer, he has visited the campuses of eight Division 1 football schools. All of these schools are offering full scholarships to the talented quarterback.

CHAPTER 1

The High School Quarterback

Trace Myers has been playing football since he was a six grader. While he was interested in other sports, the only one he preferred to participate in was football. Even at an early age, it was obvious that he was a natural at this sport. Not only was he physically talented, he also was a student of the game.

Recognizing his talent and love for the game, his family was fully supportive of him. His dad, Pete, encouraged him to be all he could be, not only on the football field but in the classroom and in life. No matter what was on Pete's schedule, he never missed one of Trace's games from the time the boy was in sixth grade.

While Trace was always a bit bigger than most of the boys he was playing with, he had an unexpected growth spurt between his sophomore and junior years. As a six-foot-two sophomore, he led the TJ Patriots to the state title. A year later, with Trace three inches taller, the undefeated Patriots repeated as state champs. By this time, he was getting national attention from many Division 1 college programs. Last winter, recruitment letters began arriving at the Myers residence from all over the country, inviting Trace to visit their campus.

Having spent all of his life on the farm, Trace planned to study in the field of agriculture. Whatever school he chose would need to have a solid agricultural program.

As the high school season grew closer, the excitement and anticipation was ramping up each day. The TJ Patriots had graduated several key players, but the nucleus of last year's championship team remained, including their blue chip quarterback.

The *Frederick News-Post* preseason report stated, "With two back-to-back state titles under their belt, we project a third title will be in Frederick at the end of the season."

This Thomas Johnson team is one of the best in this area in recent memory. Patriot's coach, Frank Luhn, is trying to downplay the past accomplishments and focus solely on this team, this season. He stated, "Barring injuries to any of our key players, I believe we can make another run for it. Keep in mind that there are other teams around the state with many returning senior players that are going to be tough competitors."

When asked if his quarterback had made a decision on where he planned to play his college football, the coach replied, "I don't think he is quite ready to commit yet. He is a mature, levelheaded young man that has many choices and is wise to consider all his options."

CHAPTER 2

Life-Changing News

Trace arrived home from practice, ready to change into his work clothes and do the cleanup in the milking barn. As he headed for his room, he passed his mother's sewing room. He heard sniffles coming from inside the room. He stopped to investigate. When he entered the room, there was his mother on her knees, praying with tears flowing down her cheeks.

"Mom, what on earth is wrong?" he asked.

Judy was not aware that Trace had entered the room and was startled to hear his voice.

Trace grabbed her arm and led her to her chair.

She looked up and said, "I'm sorry, Trace. I didn't want you to see me in this state of mind. Before I tell you what's going on, I need you to promise me that you won't tell your father what I'm about to say."

"I promise."

"Your father hasn't been feeling well for the past few weeks. I finally talked him into seeing the doctor. He had some tests done last week. Today, I went with him for his follow-up appointment. The doctor informed us that he has stage 3 colon cancer."

Trace gasped. "Oh no!" He started to cry.

"Needless to say, we were saddened by this," Judy continued, "The doctor said if there is any chance of beating this, he must begin treatments immediately. Your dad doesn't want the family to know yet because he thinks he can get the treatments, be cured, and go on with his life without anyone knowing any difference. You know he is truly a man of great faith. He believes the good Lord will see him through this. He particularly doesn't want you to know for fear that this might weigh heavy on your decision for your choice of colleges."

Trace questioned, "But, Mom, how is he going to get treatments without any of us knowing about it? I know Lori's headed back to school and Dennis is stationed in North Carolina, but how are you going to keep this from Brian who is here every day?"

Judy answered, "I spoke briefly to Brian about it while your dad was out on the tractor. He fully understands the situation and has agreed to not question why I have to take your dad to town three times a week. For the time being, the real challenge for you and Brian is to hold back your emotions and go on as if you don't know anything about this. Son, you know how much I love your father. He would be devastated if he knew I told you and Brian about this. So please, please go on with your life for now and don't let this change anything for this season or your college decision. Ask the Holy Spirit to help block this out of your mind as if you never heard it."

Trace grabbed his mother's hands and cupped his hands around hers. Together, they prayed for wisdom, strength, and self-control as they faced the difficult times that lie ahead for their family.

Later that evening, Dad, Mom, Brian, and Trace gathered for dinner. The brothers were doing their best to hide their emotions. After Brian offered the blessing, Pete asked Trace how the team was looking in practice. That kind of broke the ice for conversation.

Trace replied, "Actually, we're looking pretty good. Not sure about the defense, but the offense is practicing well. I was concerned about our running game, but it looks like Michael Trone has been working hard in the off-season. He is blowing through everyone. He's become a power runner, and I'm impressed with his moves. He told me at practice today that he wants to be part of another state champion team. I love to hear that. Even Coach Luhn mentioned how pleased he was with Michael's progress as a player and as a teammate."

Brian added, "All the local papers and even the *Baltimore Sun* has picked the Thomas Johnson Patriots to win it all again."

"Okay, next subject," Pete continued, "Have you gotten any closer to a decision as to where you plan to play college football? Everywhere I go, people ask me that question. As you know, I have never pressed you on this, but I think it's time to decide. It's really not something you want hanging over you when you begin your final high school season."

Trace and Brian's eyes met in a split second. Mom also made eye contact with Trace before he responded to his dad.

"I feel sure I will make a decision before the season starts. I've got it narrowed down to a few schools, but at this time, I'd rather not say which schools."

"Hey, that's your prerogative," Pete responded. "I assume you want to go to a school where you have the opportunity to be the starting QB in your freshman year? There are several D1 schools in need of a quarterback."

Trace replied, "I don't really feel that I have to start as a freshman. In fact, I think I might be better off observing for a year, especially at that level. You guys know as well as I do that it's a big jump from playing in Frederick County to playing in college at the Division 1 level. Also, I kind of want to concentrate on my studies during that first year. I'm sure Brian agrees from an academic standpoint. It's a big adjustment from high school to college."

Brian nods in agreement.

Pete replied, "Well, son, I've watched you play at every level. Time and time again, I have watched in amazement as you rose to the occasion. I appreciate your humble desire to learn during your first year, but please don't sell yourself short."

Mom adds, "Trace, please know that we will support your decision no matter what it is."

Trace acknowledged, "Thanks, Mom and Dad, for the encouraging words. I thank God that I am part of a family with parents that support their children in the way that you do."

Trace then turned to his brother. "Hey, Brian, did I hear you say you had to go into town this evening to pick up some things for the fence repairs?"

"Yes, I'm leaving shortly," Brian replied.

"Do you mind if I ride along?" asked Trace.

"Sure, glad to have you," said Brian.

<h1 style="text-align:center">CHAPTER 3</h1>

Brother to Brother

Trace jumped in the passenger side of Brian's pickup. Before they even got to the end of the lane, he started the conversation with Brian. "Mom told me that she talked to you about Dad's situation."

Brian replied, "I figured you knew something by the way you answered Dad's questions at the dinner table."

Trace continued, "Brian, I need your advice. Until today, I was leaning toward the University of Oklahoma. After Mom told me about Dad's health crisis, I'm considering not going to college right now until we get him through this."

Brian replied firmly, "No, Trace, that's not a good idea. First, Dad doesn't know that you know anything yet about his illness. Second, he would be very upset if you put college on hold for him. He is so excited for you and the many opportunities that you have that he never had. You need to go on with your life as planned."

Trace replied, "You know I did check out the agricultural programs at several of the universities that recruited me. Did you know that the Agricultural College at the University of Maryland ranks among the top ten in the country for numerous fields of study?"

"That doesn't surprise me," said Brian, "I can tell you that, for the four years that I was there, I was very impressed with their program. They have some dedicated instructors and excellent satellite facilities. Personally, I'm glad I chose to go there. I'm not sure it's right for you tough. Although the football program has shown some

7

promise, they are now more recognized as a basketball school rather than football."

Trace shared, "Well, in the hours today since Mom told me about this, my mind has been going 100 miles an hour. I thought that if I didn't delay college, perhaps I could go to Maryland. That way, I would be close by and could come home every weekend to be with the family. I can't bear the thought of being far away if something happened to Dad. Plus, I could help you out with some of the farm work."

"Has Maryland even recruited you?" Brian asked.

Trace answered, "They sent me a letter last winter, inviting me to visit the campus. But they never followed up with calls or firm scholarship offers like so many of the other schools did."

"I'm sure if you reached out to them and expressed interest, they would make you an offer," Brian encouraged. "I don't want to inflate your ego, but I don't know of any Division 1 school that wouldn't love to have you on their team. I do think that going to Maryland is the better alternative than putting off going to college."

Trace replied, "Thanks. I'm going to pray about this and sleep on it tonight. I may give them a call tomorrow to set up an appointment with Coach Frye. It is important that this is not made public before I tell Dad of my decision."

After parking in the supply store lot, Brian looked his brother in the eyes and said, "I will pray for you also. I know this is a very difficult situation to be in, but I trust God will lead you to the right decision."

"Thanks, brother, for the advice and the prayers," Trace responded.

CHAPTER 4

The Call and Meeting

With the news about his father weighing heavy on his mind, Trace had trouble sleeping. After his discussion with Brian and asking the Lord to guide him, he decided to reach out to Coach Frye at Maryland. He searched through all the recruitment letters he had received and found the letter from Maryland. Knowing that the coach would be at practice in the afternoon, he decided he would call in the morning.

"Good morning, Maryland Terrapins football office, this is Treena. How can I help you?"

Trace swallowed hard before he spoke. "Good morning. My name is Trace. Back in the winter, I received a recruitment letter from Coach Frye. I was wondering if he was in his office this morning? If not, could he please call me back this evening after practice? It's important that I speak with him personally."

"Well, he is in his office right now, but I'm not sure if he has time to speak with you. He has a meeting later this morning with the athletic director. Let me check with him. You say you received a recruitment letter? What was the name again?"

"Yes, this is Trace Myers."

"Okay. I'm going to put you on hold. Don't hang up. Give me a few minutes to see if he can speak with you today. He may instead choose to call you back."

"Hi, Treena. What's up?" said the coach.

"Coach, I have a young man on the phone that says he received a recruitment letter from you. He would like to speak with you about it. He said if you didn't have time this morning, you could call him back after today's practice. His name is Trace Myers."

The coach thought for a moment, *Trace Myers... Trace Myers.* "Whoa, that's the name of the quarterback from Frederick. Okay, tell him to hold on for a couple of minutes, and I will talk to him."

Coach put down the phone as his mind was racing with a myriad of thoughts. Why would Trace Myers be calling me? Finally, after regaining his composure, he picked up the phone.

"Hello, this is Coach Ron Frye. Is this the Trace Myers from Frederick, Maryland?"

"Yes, sir, it is," Trace replied.

"Well, son, what can I do for you?" asked the coach.

Trace then said, "Well, sir, before I can answer that, I need to know if you are alone with no one else listening?"

"I'm in my office all by myself," said the coach.

Trace continued, "Okay. I know this is a strange request, but what I'm about to tell you needs to be kept between you and me at least for the next week or so. Can I get your promise on that?"

Coach Frye responded with puzzlement, "Well, well, sure. I gotta tell you though, this is a surprising and very strange phone call."

Trace apologized, "I know it is, and I'm sorry for the elusiveness, but I'm in a very strange predicament. I cannot give you all the details and reasons right now, but I have decided to attend the University of Maryland, and if there is a scholarship open, I would like to play football for you."

There was a long pause at the other end of the line. The coach couldn't believe what he had just heard from the most sought-after high school quarterback in the country. He tried to control his emotions and find the right words to say.

Coach spoke, "First, let me say, shame on me. I assumed you had already committed to another school. Second, yes, we do have a scholarship available for you. I need you to know the reason I did not follow up the recruitment letter is because I didn't feel we had a chance to lure you to Maryland. With your well-documented abilities and accomplishments, I felt sure you would seek a school with a more high-profile football program. I am working hard to get us there, but we are not quite at the level of an Ohio State or LSU. I apologize for not being more aggressive with your recruitment."

"No need to apologize, coach" said Trace, "The truth is, until yesterday, I was planning on making my intentions known to attend Oklahoma. College Park is only an hour away from my home. My oldest brother graduated from Maryland. But the real deciding factor is something I cannot discuss with you on the phone. I must tell you this one-on-one, in person. Once you hear this, you will understand the whole picture. I know this is a very busy time of year for you. Could I meet you for about an hour somewhere off campus to explain this entire situation?"

Coach responded, "I'll tell you what, son. There's a real nice steak house off US 15 and Route 40 in Frederick that my wife and I visit whenever we're traveling in that area. I'll let the assistant coaches handle things, and I'll leave practice early on Thursday. Can we meet there for dinner around six forty-five? I'll treat you to a nice, juicy steak."

"Sure, I know exactly the place you're talking about. That works for me," Trace replied. "I'll see you there."

Coach Frye hung up the phone and just gazed straight ahead. He felt as though he needed to pinch himself to see if he was dreaming. Could this really be happening? What could possibly be the reason the most sought-after high school quarterback in the nation would want to play football at Maryland? How was he going to keep this to himself for several days? He wanted to call his wife, Barbara, and tell her the news, but he remembered the promise he had made to Trace. He got up from his desk, left his office, and took a long walk around the Byrd Stadium complex, trying to get his thoughts together. How was he going to tell the team? What about Jordan Pearce, his up-and-coming sophomore quarterback? How's he going to tell the athletic director.? What about the questions from the press? He mused at how one phone call on an August Tuesday morning could change his life and career. If someone like Trace Myers chose

Maryland, then how many more top-tier recruits would consider his school?

On Thursday evening, coach arrived at the steak house a little early. He requested a table somewhere in a corner away from the central dining area. When Trace arrived, the hostess led him to the table. Coach looked up from the menu and couldn't believe his eyes. Trace was a lot bigger than what he was expecting. Six feet, five inches with a near perfect physique. He got up and greeted Trace with an iron clasp handshake and motioned for him to sit down.

Trace started the conversation. "Coach, I want you to know how much I appreciate you meeting me here. This means a lot to me."

Coach replied, "Well, Trace, I want you to know I am very pleased to meet you. I've got to tell you, for the last two days since your call, I'm having a hard time concentrating on practice and the upcoming season. I hope after what I hear this evening from you can get me back into reality. Let's go ahead and order, then we can talk."

After ordering, Trace began to explain. "Coach, I come from a very close Christian family. I was born and raised on a dairy farm. My family knows what hard work is all about.

"My father, Pete Myers, is the spiritual leader of our family. Next to God, my father is the most important figure in my life. He has encouraged me in everything that I have ever done. He never played football, but he never missed one of my games. He is so pleased that I am in a position to choose from so many colleges to continue my education and my football career. You see, he never went to college, but he reflects the wisdom of God in everything he does."

"Sounds like quite a man," Coach responded.

"Indeed he is," said Trace. "My siblings and I have been blessed with wonderful parents. This past Monday, my mother informed me that my father was diagnosed with colon cancer. He is not aware that I know this. My older brother and I are the only ones who know, and we promised her we would not let on to Dad until he was ready to tell the family."

Trace continued, "I gave serious thought to putting college on hold so I could be there for him as he faced this challenge, just like he was always there for me. I know he would be very upset with me if I did that, so after looking at my options and praying about this, I decided to call you. I must be close by for my father and the rest of the family. Attending the University of Maryland was my only reasonable option."

Coach Frye paused for a moment as he marveled at what he had just heard. This put a whole new light as to why Trace had called him. He thought this must be a very special family. He had never been exposed to this kind of love and respect. "Trace, I admire you, and I must say I am envious of you. Most kids nowadays can't even imagine that kind of family life."

Trace explained, "Now that you know the reason I called, I realize this puts you in an unusual situation. I want you to know I do not want any special treatment. I am aware that Jordan Pearce is a very capable quarterback. He will be a junior when I come to Maryland. I am willing to redshirt for my freshman year."

The coach's jaw dropped literally before he spoke. "Son, are you telling me that being close by for your Dad means that much to you that you would be willing to set out your first year when you could be starting for several college programs?"

"Yes, sir," Trace replied, "You are doing me a favor by keeping this under your hat. I know of nothing to be gained for anyone to know the *real reason* for my decision. I trust you, and I wish to return that favor by not putting you in a compromising situation."

Trace continued, "It is very important that my father does not know the *real reason* why I chose to attend Maryland. So you and I need to respond to anyone who asks with the same answer. That answer is, 'Trace is seeking an agricultural degree. He likes Maryland's program over all the others he checked into. His brother graduated from Maryland's Agriculture College. He comes from a close family, and College Park is only an hour away from his home. He is redshirting because he wants to make a smooth transition to college life and Division 1 football. Yes, football is important to him, but there are other priorities in his life, such as family, education, and serving the Lord.' Can we agree that this is the answer that both of us will respond with?"

The jubilant coach responded, "I'm already rehearsing it in my mind. You've got a deal. Welcome to Maryland Terrapins football."

While it was difficult to thoroughly enjoy the meal in the midst of such an intense conversation, they finally finished. Trace signed the letter of intent. Coach took care of the check. The two of them shook hands, and much to Trace's surprise, the big burly coach gave him a hug.

Trace said to the coach, "I will be informing my high school coach and my family of this decision over the weekend. On Monday, you can then inform your athletic department and the press about this. Then we both have to brace ourselves for all the questions that are going to be thrown at us."

They both chuckled and went their separate ways. Trace was relieved that he was able to explain everything to the coach and felt confident that his secret would be kept.

Coach Frye got into his car and sat in silence, reflecting on this week and the meeting he just had. As he began driving home, he felt a unique kind of peace come over him. He couldn't wait to get home to tell his wife. He thought what an incredible young man he had just had dinner with. He felt relief that Trace was willing to redshirt and that he could now wait until Jordan Pearce's senior year for the two quarterbacks to compete for the starting job. He was glad that Trace gave him the *standard answer* for anyone who questioned why he chose Maryland. He began planning for all the hype that comes with this. He hopes that the Terrapin Boosters would not make demands for him to start Trace over Jordan next year. Now, he had a few more days to secretly ponder this and prepare mentally for the onslaught of questions that he will be hit with next week. *What a great problem to have*, he thought.

CHAPTER 5

Breaking the News

Trace finished practice Friday afternoon and requested to meet with Coach Luhn in his office.

Coach replied, "Sure, we can meet now if you wish."

The two of them walked to the school and entered the coach's office. Coach closed the door behind them and asked, "What's on your mind, Trace?"

Trace began, "Well, coach, I have made my decision as to where I want to go to college, and I wanted you to be the first person in the community to know. I will be informing my family over the weekend, so I appreciate it if you would wait till Monday to let anyone else know about this."

The coach raised both hands and replied, "You've got my word, buddy."

Trace continued, "I've decided to go to the University of Maryland. Coach Frye has given me a full scholarship. He will be making the announcement on Monday."

Coach asked with a puzzled look on his face, "Why Maryland?"

Without mentioning anything about his father's condition, Trace gave the explanation that he and Coach Fyre had agreed upon—the agricultural program, his brother being an alumni, and close to home.

Coach Luhn said, "Trace, I'm sure you put a lot of thought into this. After watching you for these past few years, not just as a football player but as a person, I have every bit of confidence in you. While I know you had many prominent Division -1 programs to choose from, I'm kind of glad you chose to become a Terp. That way, I don't have far to go to see your home games. Congratulations."

The two of them chuckled. They shook hands, and Trace thanked the coach.

Coach clenched his fist and said, "Now let's go out and win another state title for your senior year!"

Sunday afternoon, the Myers family gathered for their normal family dinner. Unlike many Sunday dinners, Dennis was home from Camp Lejeune for a long weekend, so the whole family was together. After Dennis offered the blessing on the meal, the conversation started around the table. Each family member gave an update on what was happening in their lives. Lori was pleased that she got the classes and schedule that she wanted at Frostburg. Dennis announced that he was up for a promotion to E-5 Sergeant and is taking courses with the Marine Corps Military Police. Brian gave an update on milk prices and what looks to be a promising corn harvest in the fall. He said Addison was taking care of all the wedding plans.

Pete looked at Trace with a grin. "Well, Trace, do you have anything to share with the family?"

Trace nodded and replied, "Yes, I do, but I prefer to wait until after dinner to discuss it. I'm pretty sure my news will spark some heavy conversation."

For a brief moment, things got quiet around the table, then Pete nodded in agreement and stated, "Very well then, we'll discuss that over Mom's apple pie."

As dinner was finished and Mom and Lori served up dessert, Pete again looked at Trace with a slight grin. "So, you've decided where you're going to school next year?"

"Yes, sir, I have," said Trace. "After weighing out all my options and considering everything that I am looking for in a school, I prayed that the good Lord would lead me to what he felt was best for me. It was, indeed, a very difficult decision, but I decided to accept a football scholarship at the University of Maryland."

Silence fell around the table. Trace looked around to see the expressions on everyone's face. No doubt, everyone was a bit surprised. Trace had not even informed Brian of his final decision.

Finally, Dennis broke the silence. "I'm sorry, little brother, but I don't think I understand. You have been recruited by nearly every top twenty-five football program in the country, and you chose Maryland? I'm sure you gave it a lot of thought, but I really think you would be better off with one of the more notable football schools."

Then Pete spoke up, "Like everyone else at this table, I, too, am a bit surprised about your choice. Don't get me wrong. I like Coach Frye, and I like that you won't be far away, but I agree with Dennis. Someone with your size and ability has a better chance of success when you are playing at one of the football powerhouses. So this means that, next year, you're going to be competing with the kid that took over QB last year in the middle of the season and looked pretty good?"

Trace took a deep breath before responding, "Well, Dad, the truth is, I have already informed Coach Frye that I will be redshirting my freshman year."

All the men at the table were shocked to hear this.

A puzzled father said, "Why on earth would you do that?"

Before Trace could respond, Judy spoke up, "For the benefit of Lori and I, could someone please explain what redshirt means?"

"Sure, Mom," Trace obliged. "Redshirt is a term used to describe an athlete who sets out their freshman season, allowing him to still be eligible to play on the team for the following four years. He still practices with the team, and he suits up for the games, but he sees very limited playing time during the redshirt year. A student athlete can request this status, or a coach can make this decision if he feels the athlete needs another year before he is ready to compete at the college level."

"That's a very good explanation," Pete commented, "so did Coach Frye request this, or did you make this decision?"

Trace looked lovingly at his dad. "I requested this, Dad. I'm not quite sure I'm ready for that level of competition, and I really want to concentrate on my studies and get used to college life."

Trace knew this would get a bit testy. That's why he wanted to wait until after dinner to share his news. Brian was the only one at the table who understood the decision, but he did his best to play along with the surprise announcement.

Pete was still trying to wrap his head around all of this when he said, "Son, I trust your judgment. I'm sure you thought all this out and prayed about it. So, like every other life-changing decision made by the members of this family, we will all support this choice."

At that time, Brian spoke up, "Okay, I understand your decision to go to Maryland. What I don't understand is your decision to redshirt. You could be the starting quarterback as a freshman at any number of Division 1 schools."

Pete and Dennis nodded in agreement. "I think Brian is right," Pete added, "But it's your decision."

"That's right," Mom chimed in, "It's your decision, and we are all one hundred percent behind you. We are proud of you for setting your priorities and turning to the Lord for direction. We love you. God bless you, and God bless this family."

Lori added, "Amen. Now, Trace, since you have your priorities straight, you can help me do the dishes."

Everyone laughed, except Trace, as the six-foot-five gentle giant rolled his eyes and followed Lori, his five-foot-six sister into the kitchen. What a sight!

Judy was pleased that Trace was going to college nearby, but she couldn't help but wonder if Pete's health issues played a role in Trace's decision. She felt somewhat relieved and decided not to confront Trace on the matter at this time.

That night, Trace went to bed feeling as if the world had been lifted off his shoulders. What a week it had been. Finally, everyone who needed to be told of his decision now knew and had accepted it. Only Brian and Coach Frye knew the *real reason* why he chose Maryland, and he planned to keep it that way for the time being. No one else needs to know.

He prayed, "Heavenly Father, I come before you a humble and gracious man. Thank you for guiding me through what has been one of the most difficult weeks of my life. Thank you for your wisdom and for giving me all the right words to say as I tried to do the right thing. Lord, you know how much I love my father. I ask that you hold him closely and bring him through this. Help my family to accept whatever is your will for my father. Thank you, Lord, for my wonderful, supportive family. I pray this in Jesus's name. Amen."

CHAPTER 6

A Good Problem

Early Monday morning, Coach Frye called the athletic director, Tom Patterson's office.

"Good morning, Ron," the AD answered his phone. "What's up? How's the team looking in practice?"

"Actually, with a couple of weeks to go before the start of the season, they are looking pretty good at this point," coach replied. "I am pleased with the practices and the enthusiasm. I'm really impressed with our QB Jordan Pearce. He came to camp in good shape, and his passing has improved measurably. But more importantly, he has taken on the leadership role that we all hoped he would. His teammates respect him and his work ethic. He is setting a good example for the whole team."

"That's good to hear," the AD replied.

Coach Frye continued, "Thanks, but there is something else I need to discuss with you. However, I prefer to do that in person. Would you be available to meet sometime this morning?"

"Is there a problem?" the AD questioned.

Coach replied, "Well, I guess you could say it's a problem, but it's a very good problem."

"Wow," the AD said, "I can't wait to hear about this good problem. I have a few things on my desk to complete. If you're going to be in your office, I'll stop by in about an hour."

"I'll be here," answered the coach.

When Tom arrived, the coach welcomed him into his office. Tom started the conversation, "So, tell me about this so-called good problem we have."

Coach smiled and began to explain, "Does the name Trace Myers sound familiar to you?"

The AD thought for a moment. "Yeah, that's the kid from the high school team in Frederick that's won the last two state titles. The kid that can pass with either arm. What about him?"

"Well, last week, he made his decision as to where he was going to play his college football," coach said.

"You're kidding," replied the AD. "I thought with all his credentials, he would have committed back in the spring. Okay, let me guess, it's either Notre Dame, Ohio State, or Penn State."

"None of the above," coach answered. "Trace grew up on a farm and wishes to study in the field of agriculture and resource economics. Over the summer, he checked out the programs of several of the schools that recruited him. He did his research and found that our program in this field was rated among the best. His older brother graduated from Maryland. He called me last Tuesday morning and informed me that he decided to attend the College of Agriculture at the University of Maryland. He then asked if there was a football scholarship available for him. He said he would like to play for the Maryland Terrapins."

"And your answer was?" questioned the AD.

Coach smiled and replied, "After I picked myself up off the floor, I assured him that we would have a full scholarship for him."

"How on earth did you pull this off?" asked Tom.

Coach slightly shook his head and answered, "I wish I could tell you that I aggressively recruited Trace, but that would not be true. I didn't feel we had a chance of getting him here. Other than the recruitment letter that I sent last spring, I had no contact with him until he called me last Tuesday. He's not coming here because we have a premier football program. He's coming because we have a top-ranked agricultural program. In fact, he informed me that he would like to redshirt for his freshman season so he can learn my offense and concentrate on his studies."

Tom, in disbelief, asked, "Is he that naïve that he doesn't realize what a future he has in football?"

"Naïve is not the word to describe him," coach replied, "Humble is the right word. I spent last Thursday evening with this kid, and I'm telling you I have never been more impressed with a young man his age. He is mature beyond his years. He's got his priorities in place. He's a polite and mannerly young man. He grew up in a very close-knit Christian family. Over the weekend, I called his high school coach. The coach told me that above and beyond being a great foot-ball player, he was one of the finest kids he's ever coached. He is respected by his teammates, classmates, and everyone who knows him in the community. He's the real deal."

"Okay, so how is any of this a problem?" Tom asked.

Coach answered, "The problems are going to come after we do the news release announcing this. We are going to get hammered with all kinds of questions as to how we landed this kid. We are going to be asked why he is redshirting. We need to brace ourselves to address the questions. The news release needs to be carefully worded, stating exactly what we just talked about as to the reasons he's com-ing to Maryland."

Coach continued, "Before you do the news release, I want to make the team aware of this today after practice. We can then do the release tomorrow."

"Very well," Tom agreed, "but I'm going to need your help put-ting the news release together."

Coach replied, "No problem. I'll come to your office in the morning."

That afternoon, Coach Frye called a team meeting after prac-tice. He announced to the team.

"I'm pleased to inform you that Trace Myers has made a com-mitment to attend the University of Maryland next year. For those of you who don't know who Trace is, he is a highly regarded quar-terback for the Thomas Johnson High School Patriots in Frederick, Maryland. His team has won the state title for the past two years. He will be attending the College of Agriculture here at Maryland. He plans to redshirt his first year so many of you will not have the opportunity to play with him in a meaningful setting. Tomorrow, there will be a press release announcing this, but I wanted all of you to hear this from me first."

The group sat in silence for a few moments. Finally, a young man wearing number *twelve* on his practice jersey stood up and said, "This is great news for our football program and our school. Congratulations, coach." He began to applaud and the rest of the team stood and joined in.

Needless to say, Coach Frye was touched by this. Number 12 was Jordan Pearce.

The next morning, the coach and athletic director crafted the following news release—

Tuesday August 9, 2005
University of Maryland

The Maryland Terrapins football program is pleased to announce the signing of the letter of intent from *Trace Myers*. Trace is currently a senior at Governor Thomas Johnson High School in Frederick, MD. He will be attending the College of Agriculture, studying agriculture and resource economics. Trace plans to redshirt his freshman season. He wants to take time to learn Coach Frye's offense and concentrate on his studies during that redshirt year.

Trace stated his primary reason for choosing UM was our highly regarded agricultural program. His brother Brian Myers is a 2003 graduate of Maryland's College of Agriculture.

Within minutes of the news release, the phones started ringing from the local press and media outlets. The questions were all over the place, but they were told by the athletic department that the news release was 100 percent accurate, and they would not make any further comment at this time.

CHAPTER 7

Season Wrap-Up

The Thomas Johnson Patriots went undefeated for the 2005 season. They went on to win their third consecutive state championship.

Counting the state title game, Trace Myers passed for 2,487 yards and rushed for another 510 yards in eleven games. The Patriots got national recognition by the *USA Today*, listing them among the top twenty-five high school teams in the nation.

Despite being from a midsized high school, Trace Myers was recognized on the all-USA high school players list for the second year in a row.

Meanwhile, down at College Park, the Maryland Terrapins had to deal with an overwhelming number of injuries to key players. They finished the season with five wins and six losses and missed a bowl game for the second year in a row.

Jordan Pearce was sidelined for two of the Terp's losses with an ankle injury. In the games, in which he played, he was sacked an average of five times. While he was forced to run the ball more than he wanted to, he averaged 42.4 yards, rushing, and 160.3, passing in eight games.

Coach Frye expressed his disappointment on the season and recognized that even with all the injuries, many of the losses were close games. He stated, "We have a lot of young talent on this team, and if we can stay healthy, we will again be a contender in the ACC next year."

CHAPTER 8

Pete Informs the Family

After nearly four months of treatments, Pete was not showing any improvement. He was losing weight and became weaker with each passing day. While he maintained a great attitude, his enthusiastic energy was slowly diminishing.

Over the Thanksgiving holiday, both Lori and Dennis questioned Mom about Dad's health. Judy explained, "Yes, your dad does have some health issues. You know your dad. This man of great faith feels he can overcome it, and no one has to know about it. That's all I can say for now. I'm sure when the time is right, he will be telling the family."

The Monday after Thanksgiving weekend, Judy drove Pete into town for his treatment. On their way home, Judy told Pete, "When we get home, I'm going to make a pot of coffee, and we are going to sit and have a serious talk."

Pete was pretty sure he knew what Judy wanted to talk about. He responded, "Yes, and I guess we need to pray also."

Judy was relieved to hear that her husband understood it was time to discuss this. As she reached over to put her hand on his, she said, "Yes, and to pray."

Alone in the farmhouse kitchen, the two of them sat down with their coffee. Judy began with a prayer. "Heavenly Father, thank you for the many blessings you have bestowed on our family. Thank you for always being there for us as we faced many challenges over the years. Now today, Lord, as we face this challenge, I ask that you give me the right words and that my husband, who I love so dearly, will understand my request. I pray this in Jesus's name. Amen."

Judy continued, "Pete, your children are starting to question me about your health. Over the Thanksgiving holiday, both Dennis and Lori said they noticed you had lost weight and that you weren't quite as lively as you used to be. Without showing too much emotion, I told them you were dealing with some health issues, but I wanted you to tell them when the time was right. They both accepted what I told them and asked no further questions. My dear Peter, I know you're fighting as hard as you can to beat this, and you still might. But I do feel the time has come that you need to let your family know."

Pete stared into space for a moment. Holding back his tears, he turned to Judy and said, "You are right. Before I do that, I want to see what the doctor says on the nineteenth, when I go for my next checkup. When everyone is home over the Christmas holiday, we can call a family meeting, just like we used to. Then I will give them the full report, and we can all pray together as a family."

Judy was relieved. She wasn't sure how Pete was going to react to her request. She was now certain that he had accepted whatever might lie ahead for him. Now she had to accept it herself. She reminded herself of Pete's motto: "It's all part of God's plan."

On December 19, Judy accompanied Pete to his appointment with Dr. Martin. Pete had undergone more testing and scans the previous week, and the doctor was going to go over them with Pete.

After the greetings, Dr. Martin began in a somewhat somber tone. "Pete, I'm afraid your treatments aren't working as well as I had hoped. While I do believe the treatments are slowing the spread of your cancer, they have not stopped the spread. The tests show that you now have cancer in one of your lymph nodes. I've known you for a long time, and I know you are a man of faith and you are a fighter, but I do feel it is time for all of us to face reality."

Judy was overwhelmed with sadness as the room became very quiet.

Finally, Pete spoke. "You are right, I am a man of faith. As a result of that faith, I'm not afraid of dying because I know what lies ahead for me on the other side. You are also right that I am a fighter. I intend to keep fighting this as long as I have an ounce of strength in this body. I do appreciate you leveling with me, doc. Now I need to know how long you think I have before I go home to my eternal resting place."

Doc replied, "Well, Pete, it's hard for me to predict that. Much of that depends on how quickly the cancer spreads to other lymph nodes and organs. That's why I want you to keep taking the treatments. There may also be some other forms of treatments that I might prescribe. I'm in this fight with you, but I want you to know that, as this cancer spreads, your pain and needs for medications will increase. It could be six months, or it could be as long as two years."

"Okay, doc," Pete said, "I will accept whatever is God's will, and I will cherish every minute that I have left here on earth while I look forward to the life that lies ahead."

Pete and Judy thanked the doctor and went on their way.

On the way home, Judy asked, "So you are going to tell the family next week?"

Pete replied, "Yes, but not until after we have our traditional Christmas dinner."

Later that week, Lori came home for the Christmas break, and two days later, Dennis arrived from North Carolina. With everyone home, Pete did his best to keep everyone's spirits high and reminded them of the real meaning of Christmas. Not knowing how long he had left, he soaked in the experience he had with his family.

As they were seated, ready to enjoy the feast, as was the custom for the Christmas dinner, Pete offered the blessing. "Gracious and heavenly Father, we come before you on this day as we celebrate the birth of your son, Jesus, our Lord and savior. Thank you for sending your Son to earth so that we may be forgiven of our sins. We come as your humble and grateful servants. Thank you, Father, for the abundant life we have shared as a family. We asked that you continue to bless us. Bless the food we are about to share, bless the farmers that produced it and the hands that prepared it. We pray this in the precious and holy name of Jesus. Amen."

An affirming chorus of "Amen" echoed around the table. After all the food was passed around and everyone began to enjoy the meal, Pete started the usual conversation, inquiring what was going on in everyone's life. Brian reported that there were going to be some 4-H students coming in the afternoons next week to observe and report on our modern milking process. Dennis said that he recently joined a men's Bible study group on base at Camp Lejeune—a group of six marines currently studying Ephesians. Lori reported that, during the next semester, she would be doing some student teaching at a special needs school in nearby Cumberland. Trace added that he was eagerly awaiting graduation and looking forward to his freshman year at Maryland.

Judy commented, "Wow, it sounds like there are many good things happening in your lives. Don't forget—we have Brian and Addie's wedding coming up in March."

"We have truly been blessed," said Pete, "Mom and I are so proud of all of you."

Lori spoke up. "How about you, Dad? What's happening in your life that you want us to know about?"

Pete glanced at Judy and replied, "Well, I do have something I want to share with you, but I think it's more fitting to do that with a family meeting, not here at the dinner table. Perhaps this evening after the milking is done, we can gather in the living room. Let's say around seven."

Everyone was in agreement as they anticipated that Pete was going to talk about his health status.

At 7:00 p.m., the family began to enter the living room. Pete had already thrown some logs on the fire and was seated in his favorite chair.

After all were seated, Pete began to speak: "As I looked around the table today, I realized how blessed I was to have such an incredible, loving family. What I'm about to tell you is not easy to say, but it is something you must know. Back last summer, I was diagnosed with colon cancer. At that time, I decided to get treatments with the hope that I could beat it. This is why I didn't say anything to any of you back then. Well, after my doctor's visit last week, I realized that the good Lord has different plans."

The room was silent with everyone staring at the floor, unable to speak.

Pete continued, "Doctor Martin informed me that the cancer is spreading. You, guys, know me better than anyone. You know that I do not fear death. I'm going to fight as hard as I can, but please understand that, sometime probably within the next two years, I will be leaving all of you and meeting the Lord face-to-face in heaven. I am not asking for any kind of sympathy, nor do I want you to grieve for me. I have lived a good life here on earth, and while I wish I had more days to spend with you here, I know the Lord has many more plans for me in his kingdom.

"I'm sorry to deliver this news on Christmas night. But knowing that Dennis was heading back to Carolina tomorrow, I wanted all of you to hear this at the same time."

Lori choked back her tears and said, "Dad, no matter what, we're going to *love you through this*." She then began to pray, "Dear Father in heaven. Our family comes before you this evening with heavy hearts. We ask that you wrap your loving and healing arms around our earthly father. Pull him close to you and let him know how much he is loved by all of us. While we do not always understand the disease of cancer, we do know that YOU are in control. Help all of us to accept whatever is YOUR will for this man whom we love so dearly. We pray this in the name of Jesus our Lord and savior. Amen."

One by one, each family member came forward, tearfully, to hug Pete and to reassure him of their support. As they left the room, a relieved Judy turned to him and said, "Good job, Pete."

As 2006 began, Pete continued with his treatments and maintained a positive attitude. In January, Dennis was promoted to sergeant and became a squad leader for the base military police at Camp Lejeune. Lori spent six weeks as a student teacher. Brian and Addie were married on March 11. Since Brian was now managing the entire farm operation, Pete and Judy gave them two acres of land to erect a prefab home. Trace graduated from high school in June, worked on the farm for a few weeks; he then headed to College Park to prepare for his freshman year. Over the summer, Lori and Trace gave their mother a bit of a break by driving Dad for his treatments. This allowed them to have some alone time with Pete.

CHAPTER 9

Preseason Practice

Trace arrived for preseason practice on Monday, the first week of August. The first teammate to welcome him was Jordan Pearce, the team's current starting quarterback. Jordan is an African American young man who appeared to be a natural leader. Trace was impressed by his engaging personality and the manner in which he carried himself. Jordan walked with Trace and introduced him to many of his teammates. Trace detected a bit of contention from some of the players. For some reason, several of them weren't quite as cordial as Jordan had been.

When the team mustered, Coach Frye introduced the coaching staff with a short bio on each of them. He then introduced the freshmen players and welcomed them to their first preseason camp.

All morning, the entire team worked on conditioning and wind sprints. After lunch, they broke off into groups by position. The quarterbacks split their time between the receivers and the running backs. When the time came for Trace to throw passes to the receivers, it was obvious that something was not clicking. Many of the wide-outs and tight ends were stutter-stepping or making what appeared to be intentional missteps and faulty routes, throwing off the timing, resulting in incomplete passes. Trace and the coaches seemed to be puzzled by this. To make matters worse, when any of the other QBs were passing, this didn't seem to be a problem. They were completing

90 percent of their passes. Trace walked away with his head hanging and headed for the weight room.

Jordan had observed this, but rather than making a scene on the field with Trace present, he chose to wait until they got to the locker room. He called all the receivers to gather behind a petition in a remote part of the locker room.

A befuddled Trace cut his weight routine short and returned to the locker room, just as Jordan began his talk to the receiving corps. Trace stood behind his locker and listened intently.

With a strong, loud voice Jordan began, "Look, I don't know what you guys are trying to prove but whatever it is, you need to stop right now! If you're trying to make Myers look bad, then shame on you. You guys are making yourselves look like fools. Don't get me wrong, I appreciate your loyalty, but grown men don't act like this. I'm not sure what point you are trying to make. Do you not remember that he is redshirting this year? That's by his choice."

Trace could not see who it was that asked. "Do you really believe that someone that talented is going to sit it out for a year?"

Jordan answered, "Look, I only know what the coach has told me and what Trace told me himself this morning. Besides that, what if he didn't redshirt? If he is the better quarterback, then he should be starting. I have no problem being his backup. I want what is best for our team, and I think all of you should adopt the same attitude. If you say you respect me, then make sure I never see you guys doing anything like that again. End of meeting!"

The response was positive as they stood to leave. Trace rushed out the door and waited outside for a few minutes. After a while, he entered the locker room as if he had just arrived. As he reflected on what he had just heard, he realized this Jordan guy was a true leader.

The next day, after the team got on the practice field, Trace sought out Jordan. With no one else close by, the two QBs stood face-to-face as Trace spoke. "Look, I want you to know that I cut my lifting time short yesterday and returned to the locker room when you were addressing the receiving corps. I heard every word you said, and I want you to know how much I appreciate that. You are a class act."

Jordan was shocked to learn that Trace had heard what he lectured his teammates on. He tried to recall everything that he said. He then spoke. "Hey, as a cocaptain of this team, I want what is best for every teammate. When I see contention brewing, it is my responsibility to confront it and squelch it. That's the right thing to do."

Trace again thanked him and asked, "Could we possibly get together for dinner this evening? Somewhere other than the team dining hall. I'll buy."

Jordan thought for a moment, then with a smile, he answered jokingly, "Sure, we can do that, but you don't have to buy. I have a monster appetite. I'm not sure you can afford to treat me to dinner."

They both chuckled and agreed to meet at 6:00 p.m. at an off-campus restaurant.

Upon arriving at the restaurant, they were seated at a booth. After ordering, they talked football and school. When their meal arrived, Jordan asked, "Do you mind if I ask a blessing for our meal?"

Trace responded, "By all means."

At that very moment, what Trace had suspected was confirmed. Jordan was a Christian. A brother in Christ.

As they enjoyed their meal, Trace stated, "You probably know more about me than I know about you. I see that you love the Lord just as I do. If you don't mind, can you tell me about your life?"

Jordan smiled and said, "One thing is for sure, we definitely come from different backgrounds. I know you're a farm boy from a close-knit family. My family life has been quite different, but by the grace of God, I was blessed with a remarkable mother and a loving grandmother."

As they finished up the meal, Jordan, feeling comfortable with Trace, began to share his life as if he wanted to tell the story. "I grew up in a depressed neighborhood in Baltimore. My mom went to nursing school and was an LPN at a nearby hospital. My dad worked for various different employers as a factory worker. They dreamed of someday moving out of the city into the suburbs. When I was two years old, my mother gave birth to twin girls, Janis and Jaedyn.

"Jaedyn was born with a form of autism called Asperger's syndrome. Jaedyn required attention twenty-four hours a day. My mother requested to get off of swing shifts and be assigned to strictly daywork. Given the circumstances, the hospital granted permission. My dad then took a job, working from 6:00 p.m. till 2:00 a.m. He would be home to attend to Jaedyn while Mom was working.

"After two years of caring for Jaedyn and her increasing need for attention, my father gave up.

"Mom got up one morning and found a note and an envelope on the kitchen table. Dad apologized but explained that he couldn't take it anymore. The envelope contained $600. He said he would send more money whenever he could. My mother was devastated. So I was four years old the last time I saw my dad. He never even said goodbye to me. It was hard to deal with this."

Trace was deeply touched hearing this. He couldn't imagine growing up without a father. He told Jordan, "I'm so sorry to hear this. How did you survive as a family?"

Jordan continued, "Well, it's not as bad as one would think. You see, my mother is a woman of faith. She relied heavily on the wisdom of God to guide her through the difficult times. It wasn't unusual for me to catch her praying. She took a leave of absence from the hospital and arranged to have her widowed mother move in with us. Her mother was a dear, sweet, godly lady. Between these wonderful women, they gave us a home full of love and set a great example for us. Grandma Kaye took care of Jaedyn's needs while Mom worked. Mom took night courses and, eventually, became a registered nurse. By the time I got to middle school, she was able to afford a modest house in another area of town where her family would be safer. Recognizing that I had an interest in building things and that I loved football, she enrolled me in Polytechnic Institute. That's a prep high school in Baltimore that has an advanced engineering program. It was at Poly where my desire was fed to become an engineer, and with the help of a great coach, I was able to develop my football skills. That's how I ended up here."

Trace responded, "My friend, that is quite a remarkable story. That explains why you are who you are. Thanks for sharing this with me."

Jordan added, "If you like happy endings, you'll be pleased to learn that my sister Janis graduated from high school last fall and is attending a community college. Grandma Kaye is still living at our house and is in good health. Jaedyn still requires much attention, but by the grace of God, she is attending a special needs school, and she has become more functional.

"Mom is now the nursing supervisor at the hospital. In other words, in spite of our challenges, God has blessed us in so many ways. He gives us these challenges to make us better people."

Trace nodded with a smile and said, "Amen."

The two athletes parted ways, each of them thinking to themselves that they had just found a true friend. Neither of them saw each other as Black or White. They only saw themselves as brothers in Christ.

CHAPTER 10

The Season Begins

The Maryland Terps got off to a good start. Jordan had led the team to a two and one record as they faced Wake Forest at Byrd Stadium in the fourth game. With the Terps ahead 17–10 late in the second quarter, two of the Demon Deacons defensive linemen converged on Jordan in the backfield from opposite sides. They hit him at exactly the same time for a sack. Jordan went down and was unable to get up. The medical staff rushed to attend to him. He lay on the field, motionless. As his team looked on, Trace brought them all together. "Okay, guys, we need to join in prayer for our QB."

Almost spontaneously, the entire team, coaches, and even cheerleaders went onto the field and formed a semicircle around Jordan and the medical team. All of them went down on one knee and held hands as Trace led them in prayer.

The radio broadcaster was in disbelief as he spoke into the mike. "Folks, I've been broadcasting college football for more than thirty years, and I have never witnessed anything like this. Number seventeen, freshman Trace Myers, has led the team onto the field, and they are all praying for number twelve."

He then added, "They are bringing the board out for Jordan Pearce, which implies that he has a back or neck injury." The choked-up broadcaster added, "Perhaps we should all take a lesson from these, young people, and we should also pray for Jordan."

As the collared Jordan was carefully lifted onto the board and headed for the ambulance, Trace came beside him. Jordan lifted his hand, and Trace grabbed it. Jordan softly spoke. "Thanks for the prayers."

The crowd stood and applauded as Jordan managed to give a thumbs-up before he was rolled into the ambulance. The applause continued until the ambulance disappeared.

When the game restarted, Dwayne Thomas took over at quarterback for the Terrapins. Dwayne was a junior, who had seen very little game time action, but he was next in line on the depth chart. He managed to keep the score at 17–10, going into halftime.

In the second half, his inexperience was obvious. He threw two interceptions, one for a touchdown. He was unable to get his timing down with his receivers. He finished the game only two completions on eleven attempts. The Terps lost the game 27–17 against a team that was not considered to be a powerhouse.

Collectively, Coach Frye, the team, the students, and the fans hoped that Jordan's injury wasn't as bad as it appeared. Late Saturday evening, the coach got the call. Jordan had suffered a broken collarbone and would be out for the season. The coach's heart sunk. He knew that, without Jordan, this was almost certain to be another losing season.

He immediately contacted the athletic director and gave him the bad news. There was a pause at the other end. The AD asked, "Ron, do you think there's any chance that Myers would give up his redshirt status and take over at QB?"

Coach replied, "I can't be sure of that, but I will certainly ask. Personally, I think it's our only chance of finishing with a winning season. What Trace doesn't know about our offense, he makes up for with his natural ability and physicality. I'll call him first thing in the morning before he leaves for church. I'll call you with his answer."

The AD added, "By the way, have you been watching TV news tonight? That scene of the entire team, kneeling in prayer, has been playing over and over on ESPN and all the local stations. I even saw it on one of the network newscasts. This is a good reflection on our university."

"Indeed it is," Coach replied. "I've been getting voice messages and emails all evening, expressing their concern about Jordan and letting us know what a touching scene that was. I'm very proud of our team. The presence and friendship of Jordan and Trace has had a positive impact on everybody. I'll call you tomorrow."

Around 7:30 a.m., Coach Frye placed a call to the Myer's residence. Lori answered the phone.

"Hello, this is Coach Ron Frye," he said in his toned-down voice.

"Well, hello, Coach, how are you today?" Lori asked.

"I am fine, thank you," coach answered. "Is Trace available? If so, could I speak with him?"

"Sure," she said, "he's in the kitchen. I'll get him for you."

Trace picked up the phone. "Hello, coach, I was going to call you in a bit to find out how Jordan was doing."

"Well, Trace," coach said, "I'm afraid I have some bad news. Jordan has a broken collarbone and will be out for the season."

"Oh no," sighed Trace. "Is he still in the hospital? If so, can you give me his phone and room number?"

Coach replied, "I'll have to get that for you. I have not spoken with him yet. I spoke with his mother, but I forgot to get that information from her."

Coach continued, "Trace, I need to speak with you on another matter. I know that you requested a redshirt status this season, but would you consider giving that up to become our starting quarterback?

Trace paused for a moment. He recalled Jordan's words: "You need to do what is best for the team." He understood that the other QBs didn't measure up to Jordan's skill level, and they would struggle, running the offense. He felt confident that he could do the job.

Trace then answered, "Coach, one of the reasons I chose to redshirt is because I felt we had a quality QB in Jordan. Now that he's out, if you feel you need me to take over as starting quarterback, you can count on me."

There was a noticeable sigh of relief on the other end of the line. Coach replied, "Thank you, Trace, thank you. You will start practicing with the first team offense tomorrow. We travel to Atlanta next Saturday to face Georgia Tech. They have a strong defense, so your work is going to be cut out for you."

Trace replied, "I'll be ready."

After he hung up the phone, he told his family about the coach's call and his decision. Everyone was pleased, especially Pete. He now knew that he would get a chance to see his son play college football.

Coach immediately called the AD with the good news. Tom was very happy to hear this. The news of Jordan's season-ending injury sent shock waves through Terp's Nation. But learning of Trace Myers giving up his redshirt year gave everyone a glimmer of hope.

Coach Frye spent a lot of time with the offense during the week's practices. He told Trace, "With Tech's pass rush, you are going have to get rid of the ball quickly, short backdrop and quick release. Look for your tight end twelve to fifteen yards downfield. I don't think you're going to have time to throw downfield unless you can roll out and find another receiver."

This proved to be a good game plan. The Yellow Jackets put a lot of pressure on Trace but only managed to sack him once. Trace was twenty-four for twenty-nine, passing with no interceptions. He threw for three touchdowns and had forty-one yards, rushing. The Terps won 27–23.

The Maryland Terrapins lost only two more games during the season. They finished the season with an 8–4 record. Both of their losses were close games against Miami and Boston College.

They then went to the Florida Citrus Bowl in Orlando and beat Purdue 24–7.

What could have been a disastrous season with the loss of their quarterback turned out to be a successful run, thanks to the play of Trace Myers and some excellent game preparation by the Maryland coaching staff.

At a postseason press conference, Coach Frye was asked how he was going to handle the quarterback situation next year, given the performance of Trace Myers this season and the return of Jordan Pearce for his senior year?

The smiling coach beamed. "What a great problem to have! Do you know how many coaches can only wish they had two top-tier quarterbacks competing for the starting job? We have seven months to figure it out."

CHAPTER 11

Preparing for Next Season

During the spring semester, Trace and Jordan stayed in touch and met for dinner a couple of times. Jordan was recovering well and hoped to be ready for preseason camp. They never really spoke too much about football. Most of their discussions were about their classes, their families, and their plans for the summer. Their friendship had grown through their common love for the Lord. Jordan was able to get an internship for June and July at an engineering firm in Baltimore County. Of course Trace would be working on the family farm.

On Monday, the week before classes were to end, Trace received a message from Coach Frye, requesting a meeting in his office whenever it fit his class schedule. Trace told him he could be there on Wednesday at 1:00 p.m.

On Wednesday, he arrived at the agreed time. When he entered the coach's office, he was surprised to see Jordan seated in front of the coach's desk. They exchanged greetings and Trace asked, "What's up?"

Coach put his elbows on the desk and said, "Jordan has something he wants to share with you. He is proposing something that he feels is best for our team. I'll let him do the rest of the talking."

Jordan cleared his throat and began, "After seeing what took place last season, I don't think that there is any question that you are the best quarterback on this team. I was never a good passing QB. I have always had much more confidence running the ball than I did passing. In fact, I don't know if I ever told you this, Trace, but I was a running back at Poly until my junior year. That's when they asked me to move to QB. I had success there because I could run. As you know, our tailback and fullback are both graduating, leaving a real void of experience in the backfield for the upcoming season. What I have suggested to coach is to let me move to running back and you become the full-time starting quarterback. With your ability to pass with either arm, scramble, roll out, and throw downfield, this puts our team in a better position to win. In addition, with me in the backfield, it also allows us to get creative with the offense. Using the pistol formation will create more confusion for our opponent's defense. How do you feel about this?"

Trace was surprised by this whole proposal. Before he could give an answer, he asked, "What about your collarbone? You don't want to reinjure that."

Jordan responded, "I don't think there's any greater chance of that as a running back as there is at QB. After all, that's the position I was playing when the boys from Wake Forest decided to make a QB sandwich out of me."

They all chuckled. Trace commented, "I hope you're not doing this just because we are friends?"

Jordan replied, "I'm not. I'm doing this because it is what's best for our team. I don't have any visions of ever being drafted by an NFL team. Personally, I think if we do this, the sky is the limit for this team next season."

Trace looked at coach. "Do you feel as good about this as we do?"

Coach smiled and replied, "I sure do. I think it's a great idea. Because of you, guys, I've never felt better about our team. Now my question to you is, Do we let this plan out now, or do we wait until preseason practice?"

Jordan said, "I think we wait and keep everyone speculating."

Trace added, "I agree. No one really needs to know at this point."

"Okay," Coach agreed. "But one more thing. I don't want anyone to think this was my idea. Jordan, you are respected by your teammates and our fans. I believe if I report that you came forward with this suggestion, they will believe it because they know the kind of person you are. I simply don't want anyone to think I pushed you into this."

Jordan understood the coach's concern. He replied, "Don't worry, coach, I think anyone who is a true Terps fan will agree this is the right move."

Trace chimed in, "Man, I can't wait until the season starts."

Jordan said, "Hold on, I've got to get this collarbone healed and get back in shape."

They all laughed.

Coach added, "I can't wait either. We've got something special here. Thank you, gentlemen."

The coach escorted the two athletes to the door. As he closed the door behind him, this father of three daughters thought of how proud he would be to have either one of those guys as his son. He thought also of how fortunate he is to have both of them on the same team.

CHAPTER 12

Jordan Visits the Farm

When Trace arrived home on Friday evening after his final week at school, Pete was sitting on the porch in his favorite rocking chair. During the past season, Pete was only able to get to two of the Terp's home games. His deteriorating health prevented him from doing much traveling. With the help of his wife and children, he still managed to get to church on Sunday mornings. This was something that was very important to him.

Dr. Martin had recently changed his treatments, which lessened his posttreatment exhaustion and pain. He was no longer capable of doing any of the labor work around the farm but did as much as he could with the administrative part of the business.

When Trace got out of the car, his dad gave him a smile and a wave. "So you're going to be home for a couple of months?"

Trace responded with a thumbs-up, climbed the porch steps, and gave his dad a big hug as they exchanged verbal greetings, then sat down next to him and started to share the news. "Dad, you'll never guess what happened this week."

Pete responded, "Well, judging by the tone of your voice, it must have been something good."

"Yes, it is," said Trace. "Jordan Pearce has recovered well from his injury. He went to Coach Frye and requested to be moved to the running back position. As you know, Jordan is a Christian and is very unselfish. Since the day I met him, he has always wanted what was best for the team. The coach agreed with Jordan's suggestion. That means that there is no competition between me and my best friend for the starting quarterback job. I am now the first-string quarterback."

"Wow, this is very good news," Pete exclaimed. "This kid must be a well-grounded young man."

"Indeed he is," said Trace, "He was brought up in the city. He comes from a broken family but with strong Christian values. He walks closely with the Lord."

"You know, I would like to meet this young man," said Pete. "Why don't you invite him to join us for Sunday dinner sometime soon?"

Trace thought for a moment and said, "I think that would be good. I doubt that he has ever been on a farm. Knowing him, he would look at it as a learning experience. I'll give him a call to invite him."

Trace shared his news with the rest of the family, along with Dad's idea to have Jordan for Sunday dinner. They all agreed it would be nice to have him as a dinner guest and looked forward to meeting him.

Mom cautioned Trace, "Just let me know when he is coming so I can have enough food for an extra football player at the table."

Over the weekend, Trace made the call to Jordan. After the greetings, Trace said, "My family asked me to call to invite you to Sunday dinner with us sometime this summer. They have heard me speak of you and our friendship and would like to meet you. I thought, too, that you might enjoy seeing what life is like out here on the farm."

Jordan thought for a moment and said, "You know, I think I would really like that. How about the Sunday before July 4 holiday?"

Trace said, "That works for us. Let me give you the exact address. Try to be here between noon and one o'clock. Mom's a stickler for serving dinner at one on Sundays."

"Sounds good," Jordan replied, "I'm looking forward to meeting your family."

When Jordan arrived, Trace went to greet him in the driveway. After exchanging hellos, Trace said, "Before you meet my family, I need to let you know something. My dad is battling cancer. The treatments have caused him to lose weight and stamina. His mind is still good, but he is frail. You don't need to bring it up unless he does. I just thought I would warn you in advance."

Jordan acknowledged, "I understand."

Trace introduced Jordan to the family. His dad (Pete) and his mom (Judith), his brother Brian and his new bride, Addie, and his sister Lori. He explained his brother Dennis was stationed in North Carolina.

Pete spoke up. "We are very pleased to meet you. Trace speaks very highly of you."

Jordan replied, "I am very pleased to meet all of you. My buddy here has told me what a great family he has. Thank you for inviting me."

At 1:00 p.m., they all gathered around the big dining room table. Jordan marveled at all the good, fresh food on the table. After everyone was seated, Judy offered the blessing. "Heavenly Father, we thank you for this beautiful day. Thank you that we can gather as a family and enjoy your bounty. We welcome Jordan to our home and pray that you continue to bless his life as he walks closely with you. We pray that you do the same for all of our family. Bless the food we are about to share, the farmers that produced it, and the hands that prepared it. We pray this in Jesus's name. Amen."

After all the food was passed around and everyone was enjoying their meal, Pete began the conversation. "So, Jordan, how's your collarbone healing? We were watching the game that day when you took that hit. I think all of us grimaced when we saw the replay."

Jordan replied, "I'm now finished with therapy. They have put me on a rigorous fitness program to help me regain my strength." Jordan looked around the table with a smile and said, "As dairy farmers, you'll be pleased to know that I'm drinking more milk now than I ever have in my life. I need that calcium to strengthen my bones."

Everyone around the table smiled and nodded with approval.

Pete continued, "Trace tells me you are in the engineering program at Maryland. What type of engineering are you looking to get into?"

Jordan answered, "I'm concentrating on civil engineering. I would like to design and build highways, bridges, and tunnels. I have always been fascinated by transportation byways. I admire Dwight Eisenhower for spearheading the development of our country's interstate highway system."

Brian spoke up. "That sounds interesting. You shouldn't have any problem finding employment in that field, given the current status of our country's infrastructure."

Jordan nodded in agreement. "For sure! That's exactly why I became interested in the field. I see the conditions of our streets and highways and want to do my part to improve them."

After dinner and dessert, the men made their way to the front porch. Jordan turned and said, "Thanks, Mrs. Myers, for that great meal. You all sure know how to eat well."

Judy acknowledged with a smile. "Thanks, Jordan, but I had help from Lori and Addie. We are all so glad you could join us."

Pete then suggested, "Trace, why don't you take Jordan on the Gator (utility vehicle) and show him around the farm?"

Trace agreed, and the two athletes piled into the Gator and took off. When they pulled up to the Tractor shed, Jordan looked at Trace and asked, "How long ago was it when your dad was diagnosed with cancer?"

Trace replied in a solemn voice, "It was almost two years ago, right before my senior year of high school."

Jordan paused, then noted, "So that's the *real reason* you decided to come to the University of Maryland?"

Trace dropped his head and stared downward as he admitted, "Yes, that is the real reason, but Dad doesn't know that. He was surprised when I told him I was going to Maryland. As far as he knows, I decided on Maryland because of their agricultural program. Only my brother Brian, Coach Frye, and, now, you know that this is why I made the decision. My dad would be very upset with me if he knew that he was the reason I turned down the other offers. He must never know. You see, my dad has always supported me in everything I ever did. He is my hero, and I love him dearly. It was important that I be nearby to support him during his health crisis. No football future or education could ever overshadow my love for that man."

An emotional Jordan replied, "I'm so glad I came here today. You have been blessed with a wonderful family, and it's pretty obvious that everyone has respect and admiration for your dad. One of the Ten Commandments is *'Honor your father and your mother so they may live long in the land of the Lord, your God, is giving you.'* It warms my heart to see that you and your siblings are doing just that."

Jordan continued, "Now that I know the *real reason* you chose Maryland, I have even greater respect for you. You have my word that I will not share this with anyone. I understand why you had to tell Coach Frye because I'm sure he questioned your decision."

Trace replied, "Yes, I had to tell him. To his credit, he has kept his word and to my knowledge, has never told anyone else."

The two of them continued the tour of the farm and ended up in the milking facility where Brian was preparing the equipment. Jordan was impressed with the entire farming operation.

As they returned to the farmhouse, Jordan said his farewells and thanked everyone again for having him.

Trace walked Jordan to his car. Before their farewell, Trace told Jordan, "Now that you know the whole story, I want you also to know that I have no regrets on my decision. I am close to home, I'm in a good agricultural program, and in you I met a true brother in Christ, and our football team has a promising future. As Dad would say, 'it was all part of God's plan.'"

Jordan smiled and agreed. "I think you are right. Thanks again. See you in August."

CHAPTER 13

The 2007 Season

On the first day of preseason camp, Coach Frye had his traditional team meeting, introducing the coaches and all the new players.

The coach addressed the team. "Given all that we had to deal with last year, I think we surprised a lot of people with our successful season and the bowl championship. For those of you who were on that team, I want to again thank you from the bottom of my heart for stepping up in the way that you did. With that, I want all of you to know that I am even more optimistic about this season. I believe we have the nucleus here to accomplish great things. You might ask, 'Why do you feel this way, Coach?' Well, to better explain that, I'm going to turn the meeting over to your cocaptain, Jordan Pearce. Welcome back, Jordan."

Jordan moved to the front of the room and began with, "Go, Terps! The reason Coach wanted me to address you is because I believe that what I am about to share is something that is going to have a dramatic impact on the success of our season. When I got injured last year, I was deeply touched by your show of support as you came onto the field and kneeled in prayer for me. It was then that I realized that I was part of something very special. It was also a positive reflection on our university."

Jordan continued, "During those next few months as I recovered, I watched this team come together in a way that I think few could have anticipated. I join with the coach to let you know how proud I am of this group. As you know, as one of your captains, it is always my intent to do what needs to be done for the success of this team. Having said that, considering that I have always been more of a running QB, I believe it is best that I move to the running back position and fill the void left in our backfield. We have in Trace Myers, a multidimensional quarterback, who is a very capable leader of our offense and in whom I am pleased to share the field with. With this move and our improving defense, I believe we can win the conference and stand toe to toe with any of the elite teams in the country. Now, let's go show the world what the Terps are capable of!"

The entire team, including coaches, stood with applause and jubilation with high fives as Jordan left the platform.

The enthusiasm filled the room as Coach Frye returned to the platform and yelled over the noise, "Now you know why I'm so optimistic! Now let's go out there and get to work!"

News of the retooled Terps backfield spread quickly among the fan base and the college football community.

The Terps began the season, ranking twenty-third in the nation by the AP Poll. After stunning wins over number 4 West Virginia and number 10 Rutgers, they climbed into the top 5 in the poll in week six of the season. Opposing teams couldn't stop the Myers-led offense. They closed out their undefeated season with decisive wins against number 8 Boston College, Florida State, and North Carolina State. They ended their regular season at number 2 in the AP Poll and qualified to play against number 1 Ohio State in the BCS National Championship Game at the Louisiana Superdome on January 7, 2008.

The excitement around campus and among the alumni was fever pitch. Coach Frye did everything he could to keep his team out of the hype and focused on the business at hand.

Trace Myers finished second in the voting for the Heisman Trophy.

Meanwhile, back in Frederick County, the Myers family was filled with joy. Pete was so happy to watch his son lead the Terps to an undefeated season.

A close friend of the Myers family (Kellie), who is an RN (registered nurse) and wife to another dairy farmer, had a connection with a nearby family-owned snack food company in Hanover, Pennsylvania. This company is also a sponsor of Maryland athletics and has a strong share in the Baltimore/Washington market. Through her connection, she was able to set up a meeting with the company's executive vice president to make a special request.

During that meeting, she explained the plight of the Myers family, their standing in the community, and the health issues of Pete. She explained the closeness of the family and how Pete never missed one of Trace's games until he went away to college. She then asked the EVP if it would be possible to donate the use of the company jet and pilot to fly Pete and the rest of the Myers family to New Orleans for the National Championship, stating that it could be the last game Pete Myers would ever see his son play. She went on to request that, if approved, they would like to keep this among a close circle until after the game. "I don't want Trace to know that they are going to be there, for fear it might impact his game." Kellie continued, "I've known this family for a long time. I can think of nothing that would mean more to them than this. I will take care of all of the other arrangements. I will even provide your pilot with all his meals. All I'm asking of your company is to donate the use of your plane and the pilot."

The EVP replied, "I don't know if you know this, but I have a daughter that is a sophomore at Maryland. She has told me of the excitement surrounding the football team. She is in a class with Trace Myers and speaks of what a humble and kind person he is. I can see your passion for this. They must be quite a family. I will reserve the plane and the pilot for January 7. I will send my approval to our pilot. Here is his name and number. You must coordinate everything with him."

Kellie was nearly in shock that the EVP had so easily granted her request. She replied, "Thank you, thank you. You have no idea what this means to the family and to me. I assure you that you will never regret this. You have done a great service to a remarkable family."

Before leaving Hanover, Kellie called the Myers' home. Judith answered.

Kellie asked, "Judy, would it be okay if I stopped by in about an hour? I have something I need to talk to you and Pete about."

Judy answered; "Sure, you know you're welcome here anytime."

"Okay, I'll see you in a little bit," said Kellie.

When Kellie arrived at the farm, she sat down with Pete and Judy. She began to explain, "There is a company in Hanover, Pennsylvania, that has offered the use of their company plane and a pilot to fly your entire family to New Orleans for the National Championship on Monday, January 7. I have already contacted the Maryland Athletic Department, and they are providing us with complimentary tickets for your family and myself. The game begins at seven thirty, Central time. I will take you in my van to the Westminster airport. I will be flying with you to take care of Pete's medical needs, medications, and wheelchair. We will leave Westminster around 2:00 p.m. It will be a late night, so you might want to sleep in that morning. We will leave after the game and should return to Westminster around 1:30 a.m. What do you think about this?"

Pete and Judy looked at each other with puzzled looks on their face.

Judy asked, "Why would they do this for us?"

Kellie answered, "Well, for one thing, they know what a great family you are. They are a sponsor of Maryland athletics. Plus, the executive VP has a daughter at Maryland, who is in one of Trace's classes. By the way, we can't let Trace know anything about this until after the game. I think it is best that we keep this as a surprise."

Judy turned to Pete, "Do you think you can handle that kind of travel schedule?"

Pete nodded affirmatively. "To see our son play in the National Championship, I believe God will give me the strength I need to be there in person. After all, I am retired and can sleep all day the next day. Plus, I will probably be able to get some sleep on the plane. I say, let's do this!" Pete's eyes were filled with tears of joy.

Judy smiled at Nurse Kellie and said, "I don't know how you pulled this off, but I want you to know how much this means to us, especially to this guy. I will let Brian and Addie, Lori and Dennis know about this. We will be ready. Thank you so much." Judy wiped away her tears.

Just then, Brian walked in.

Kellie spoke up. "Hello, Brian, I'm glad you are here. Your parents will fill you in on the whole story, but for now, all you need to know is that your entire family is going to the National Championship in New Orleans on January 7. I have here a chart that shows where we will be sitting. I was wondering if you could contact Coach Frye and let him know that we are going to be there. We don't want Trace to know anything about this."

Judy added, "In fact, the only other person that should know about this is Jordan Pearce. He is a captain on the team. He and Trace have become close friends. We've had him here for dinner. He knows our family. I know he would be happy that we will be there."

A confused Brian replied, "Okay, I'm not sure how all this came about, but I will call the coach and ask him to let Jordan know."

Kellie added, "Brian, if you can do the morning milking that day, Chuck can come over and take care of the afternoon duties."

Brian replied, "Sounds great to me. Thank you."

After Kellie left, Pete and Judy filled Brian in on the entire plan.

Brian exclaimed, "This is great! The only thing that can make this better is if Maryland wins. Dad, are you sure you can handle this?"

Pete responded, "Son, knowing that I will be with God and family gives me the confidence that I can do this."

CHAPTER 14

The Championship Game

On the morning of the game, January 7, Trace called home from New Orleans.

When Pete answered, Trace said, "Hi, Dad, I wanted to call now because we will be in drills off and on all day today. I wasn't sure if I would get a chance to call later."

Pete replied, "I understand. How's the weather down there?"

Trance answered, "Right now, it's a bit humid. Temperature is seventy-one degrees. Of course we're playing in the dome tonight, so the weather shouldn't be a factor. That place is huge. I wish you and Mom could be here tonight."

Pete cautiously replied, "Yes, I wish we could be there, but you know I never did travel well. Rest assured, we will be there in spirit. I just want you to know we are very proud of you."

"Thanks, Dad," Trace said, "Ohio State is a good team, but I think if our receivers can get open, we can beat them."

"Good luck, son." said Pete, "Stay strong, keep the faith, and God bless you."

After they said their goodbyes, Trace thought how he wished his mom and dad could be there. Back home, Pete smiled and said to himself, "I can't wait to see the look on his face when he finds out we were there for the whole game, not just in spirit but in person."

Kellie arrived in the van at 1:00 p.m. The Myers family was ready. Dennis took an extra-long weekend. Lori was still home for semester break. They got settled in the van while Kellie loaded Pete's wheelchair in the back. They arrived at the airport in plenty of time. The pilot had the plane ready and was prepared to board his special passengers. The pilot took care of storing the wheelchair while Kellie and the family got settled on the plane. Then off they went to New Orleans.

When they arrived at a municipal airport outside of New Orleans, Kellie had arranged for a shuttle bus to pick them up. They were all soaking in the sights of the city as they approached the superdome. The shuttle dropped them off at the gate they needed to go in. They made their way to the seats. The seats were at the top of the lower level in the handicapped section with plenty of room for Pete's wheelchair. The rest of the family had seats adjacent to him.

All of them watched intently to see if they could see big number 17 out on the field, warming up.

Pete was in his glory, constantly glancing around the magnificent surroundings.

Suddenly, Dennis said, "There he is!" The entire family focused on the sideline as Trace was throwing soft passes.

Judy said, "I hope he doesn't look up here and see us."

"Are you kidding?" Brian exclaimed, "He's so focused on this game he doesn't know there are any fans here. You all know Trace well enough. When it comes to game day, he's all business."

During warm-ups, Lori noticed number 12 Jordan Pearce, on the sideline, scanning the seats, looking for the Myers family. Lori and Addie stood up and waved to him. Jordan waved back to acknowledge the location of the group.

Following the pregame hoopla, the teams came out of their respective tunnels to the cheers of their fans. Number 12, Jordan Pearce, led the Terrapins onto the field. It actually seemed like the cheering was louder for the Terps than it was for the Buckeyes. The crowd noise was at fever pitch as Maryland kicked off to Ohio State.

The Maryland defense was nearly flawless as they held the Buckeyes to just three points in the first quarter. Trace threw for one touchdown, and Jordan ran for a nine-yard touchdown. They added a field goal in the second quarter.

With the score 17–3 late in the second quarter, the Ohio State fullback was lead, blocking for the tailback when he somehow got tangled up with one of his own lineman. Number 49 was a three-year starter for the Buckeyes and a respected senior cocaptain. As he went down, he was holding his right leg. It was obvious he was in great pain. The medical staff rushed out to attend to him as seventy-five thousand spectators looked on with quite respect. It appeared as if he might have broken his leg.

Almost spontaneously, the Maryland team gathered on the sideline and followed Trace Myers and Jordan Pearce onto the field. In unison, they all kneeled to pray. Across the field, the Buckeyes team was also gathering as they, too, came out onto the field and kneeled.

The TV broadcaster spoke with a trembling voice, "Ladies and gentlemen, take good look at what's taking place down on the field. Coach Frye has something very special going on at Maryland. This isn't the first time his team has done this. But this time, it's for a player on the opposing team, and it's on national TV. For those of you who think that today's kids are the *me* generation that doesn't care about others, then I want you to take a long, hard look at this scene. Soak it in. If that doesn't make you proud to be an American, then I don't know what will."

The Buckeyes fullback was taken off the field on a stretcher with an apparent broken leg. The seventy-five thousand people in attendance stood with respective applause for the fallen Buckeye. The two teams, kneeling in prayer, sparked tears and emotional feelings throughout the stands and for the millions watching on TV.

Pete was also in tears as he thought how proud he was that his son was part of that remarkable gesture of sportsmanship.

The game continued. Ohio State managed another field goal before halftime. The Terrapins also added a field goal, giving them a 20–6 lead at the half.

As the second half began, it was obvious the Terps were smelling victory. Following the second half kickoff, they marched down the field, and Trace found his tight end in the end zone, adding another touchdown.

After a couple of three and outs by both teams, the Buckeyes did manage to get a touchdown, making the score 27–13 at the end of the third quarter.

In the fourth quarter, Ohio state came fighting back with another touchdown and a successful two-point conversion, cutting the Maryland lead to 27–21. With less than four minutes left in the game, the Terps were in the red one. Trace faked a handoff to Pearce, then rolled to his left with Buckeye defenders chasing him. Suddenly, he saw number 12 standing in the end zone. While in the grasp of two Buckeyes, with his left arm, he threw a perfect pass to Pearce. This all but sealed the game for the Terps.

With the Terps up 34–21, the Maryland defense just completely shut down Ohio State's offense.

The Terps got the ball back for a few running plays, then ran out the clock. For the first time since 1953, the Maryland Terrapins are College Football's National Champions.

The Maryland fans poured onto the field as the teammates celebrated with hugs and high fives.

Amid all the jubilation, Jordan sought out Trace and led him to the sideline. Jordan pointed toward the stands and said, "I want you to look up to the top of the lower-level seats. There are some folks up there that would like to congratulate you."

Trace peered to where Jordan pointed and saw his dad in a wheelchair surrounded by his family as they were frantically waving to him. Tears filled his eyes, and he took off running to a nearby opening in the wall. He ran up the steps then dropped to his knees in front of Pete. An emotional Pete placed his frail hands on Trace's cheeks and looked him in the eyes and said, "See, son, I told you that you could do this."

Trace stood and greeted and hugged the rest of his family. An emotional Trace then said, "I want all of you to know that winning the national championship is great, but knowing that you were here makes it even better and means so much more to me."

Kellie spoke. "We are flying back to Maryland tonight. I'm sure this surprise will be explained to you the next time you call home."

Trace shook his head and said, "I can't wait to hear how all of this came about. I must now join Coach Frye and the rest of the team down on the field for the trophy presentation. Thank you so much for being here. I love you, guys. Have a safe flight back."

For the rest of that night and all of the next day, the news was filled with highlights from the game. The Maryland Terrapins's football team was not only being heralded as the national champs but being held up as a model for all college sports. The sight of an entire team praying for an opposing team's player was replayed as often as the actual game highlights.

Social media and talk shows were flooded with positive comments on the incredible display of concern and sportsmanship shown at the game.

When Trace called home the next morning, his mom told him they didn't get to bed until three fifteen that morning, and Pete wasn't up yet. She then went on to explain the events that took place that led to them coming to New Orleans.

In the ensuing months following the championship game, it was obvious that the Maryland Terrapins's football team had won more than the national title. They also won the hearts of countless college football fans across the country. If you were to ask even the most loyal, die-hard fan of any college who their second favorite team was? The majority of them would answer, The Maryland Terrapins.

CHAPTER 15

Pete's Final Days

Following the championship, things returned to normal for Trace. He came home every weekend. Each week, he could see his father getting weaker and weaker. His mom told him that the cancer was found in more lymph nodes. Individually, the entire family was praying for Pete. Trace asked God to spare his father of severe pain.

As the winter drew to a close and the fields and trees began to turn green, it was obvious that Pete would not be with them much longer. He was unable to get out of bed without assistance.

During the second week of April, Brian and Addie welcomed a baby girl into the world. This was Pete and Judy's first grandchild. When she was a week old, they took little Ellie to see her grandfather. Pete beamed with pride as they laid her next to him. "So this is the beginning of the next generation of our family. What a precious little girl. Welcome to our family, Ellie."

By the end of April, Pete's pain had increased to the point where he needed pain medicine constantly. Dr. Martin came to visit him at the farm. He prayed with him and wished him farewell. The doctor told Judy he was calling in hospice.

Judy called Dennis, Lori, and Trace and told them the sad news. They all headed home to be there for their Dad's final hours.

Trace informed his instructors, Coach Frye, and Jordan.

Dennis put in for emergency leave and informed his Bible study group that he would not be around for a week or so. He asked for prayers for his family. Through this Bible study, Dennis had made friends with Gunnery Sergeant Tom McNickle. Tom was a faithful follower of Christ. He and Dennis had become prayer partners and met frequently for lunch. Tom served on the base color guard unit as a bagpiper. He told Dennis to keep him posted and to let him know when the services would take place. He then went to his commanding officer with a special request.

Captain Fischer welcomed Tom into his office and asked, "What's on your mind?"

Tom began, "Captain, I have a very close friend, a fellow marine, who is a brother in Christ, whose father is on his deathbed. His dad never served in the military, so I know he doesn't qualify for a full military service. He has been a farmer all his life. He is a devout Christian. He and his wife have raised four kids and have brought them up to be godly people. In fact, if you are a football fan, their youngest son was the quarterback for the Maryland team that won the national title. What I'm asking for is your permission to attend the funeral in Maryland in full uniform and to use the Marine Corps bagpipes for the ceremony. I will take personal leave when I learn of the date."

The captain asked, "Who is this marine you wish to do this for?"

Gunny answered, "His name is Sergeant Dennis Myers. He is a squad leader for the base military police."

Captain Fisher responded, "I know Sergeant Myers. He's a very fine marine. But I didn't know that was his brother that did so well against Ohio State. I've heard a lot about that kid, how he shocked everyone by choosing to go to Maryland. Okay. You have my permission to attend the funeral in full Marine Corps dress blues, and you have my permission to use the bagpipes. I will have this all typed up for you. But you do not have my permission to use your personal leave time. Once you learn the date of the service, let me know, and I will issue a three-day pass, allowing for a day of travel time to and from Maryland."

Gunny McNickle stood with a big grin and saluted the captain. "Thank you very much, sir."

Captain Fisher smiled, returned the salute, and dismissed the gunny.

After a six-hour drive from Camp Lejeune, Dennis arrived home. He immediately went to his father's bedside. Pete smiled and said, "I'm so glad that you made it home in time so I could tell you how much I love you and how proud I am to call you my son." Pete then pointed to some folded papers on a nearby table. He said, "Son, if you are able, I ask that you read that note at my funeral service."

Without even looking at the contents of the note, Dennis promised to fulfill his father's request. The big tough marine was in tears as he turned to leave the room.

The following Saturday morning, Pete knew it was time to leave this earth and go home to be with his Lord and Father in heaven. No more pain. No more tears. The family gathered around his bed. He spoke a soft farewell to each of them individually. He then took Judy's hand, and as his voice grew so weak that he had to take a breath nearly every three words, he said, "God sent you to me to be my soul mate and best friend. And you have been that and so much more. Thank you for always being there for me. Thank you for the wonderful life we have shared." With that, he closed his eyes, and a few minutes later, he drew his last breath.

Needless to say, every family member was crying, but they were also at peace because they knew where Pete was going to be from now for eternity. He was no longer in pain.

Trace later called Coach Frye and Jordan to tell them about Pete's passing. They both gave their condolences.

Dennis called his commanding officer to let him know that he wouldn't be back until late next week. He also called his friend Tom McNickle to make him aware of his dad's passing.

The following Monday morning, they went to the funeral home to make arrangements. As they anticipated a large number of people would be attending, it was decided that it would be best to have the services at Pete's church. A viewing would be held at the funeral home on Wednesday. Then on Thursday, the family would receive friends from 10:00 a.m. to 11:00 a.m. at the church with the service starting at 11:00 a.m.

Coach Frye contacted Trace and asked for the date, time, and location of the service. He said he and his wife planned to attend.

Down at Camp Lejeune, Tom McNickle went on line to obtain the information for the service. He then notified Captain Fischer. As promised, the captain granted a three-day pass for Tom to attend.

The viewing on Wednesday was supposed to end at 8:00 p.m. However, there were so many people wanting to pay their last respects to Pete that it was nine forty-five when the last group filed through. Judy was exhausted.

Thursday was a beautiful, bright, sunshiny day with very little wind and temperatures expected to be in the low seventies by noon.

The family arrived at the church at nine forty-five Thursday morning and took their place at the rear entrance of the worship center, preparing to greet those who came to attend the service. Trace, being the youngest in the family, would be the first in line to greet the guests with Judy being at the end of the line of family members. A group of young adults, who had been mentored by Pete and other members of the Myers family through 4-H and FFA, had volunteered to serve as pallbearers. Pete's closed casket was positioned in front of the altar.

People began arriving before 10:00 a.m. A steady stream of friends from throughout the community filed into the church. At about ten fifteen, two charter buses pulled onto the church parking lot. More than sixty players and coaches from the University of Maryland football team came off the buses and gathered as a group. Coach Frye, who had driven separately, met them and thanked them for being there.

Coach Frye and his wife, Barbara, entered the church first and expressed their sympathy to each member of the family. Trace then turned to find his friend and teammate Jordan Pearce, standing in the doorway. After Jordan hugged his buddy, he pointed to the line behind him and said to Trace, "They wanted to be here for their QB."

Trace had trouble holding in his emotions as he greeted each of his teammates and coaches. The other family members were deeply moved by the show of support for their family. The team filled the two back rows of seats. By this time, the worship center was nearly at full capacity. When some of the later arrivals couldn't find a seat, a number of the football players gave up their seats and stood in the back of the room.

The service began as Pastor David greeted the large gathering and offered a prayer. Everyone in attendance was asked to join in singing some of Pete's favorite hymns. Brian and Lori read from Scripture the verses that Pete had requested. Pastor David read the official obituary and spoke of Pete's life accomplishments. He then invited anyone who wished to come forward to speak about the beloved gentleman. A number of people came forward. They spoke of how Pete had made such a positive impact on them. They spoke of his integrity, his credibility, his love for his family, his desire to help others, his work ethic, his generosity, his passion to help young people learn about farming, his steadfast love for the Lord, and his desire to share the gospel with others.

As the last person paid tribute and left the podium stand, Sergeant Dennis Myers stood and came forward in his marine dress blue uniform. Pete's second son began to speak. "On behalf of our entire family, I wish to thank all of you for being here today to honor my father. Thank you for the many kind words spoken here today."

He continued, "Two days before my dad's passing, he asked me if I would read a message he wanted to share during his funeral service. As you know, any of us kids would do anything for our dad. So without reading the note, I promised my father I would read it during the service. Later, after I read the message, I knew that I might struggle getting through it, so I asked my brother Brian if he would rescue me if I got too choked up. So if you see Brian bail me out, you'll know it was planned that way."

This is the message my Father wanted me to deliver:

> Greetings to all. As you know, I have always
> walked closely with the Lord. When I learned
> of my health challenge, I accepted it as part of
> God's plan. While I may be leaving this earth at
> a relatively young age, I realize that I have been

blessed with a full and abundant life. So please don't grieve for me.

I accepted the Lord into my life when I was eleven years old. From that time forward, I trusted him to lead me in everything I do. He sent me a wonderful wife to spend my life with. He gave us four healthy and happy children for whom we raised in a godly home. He provided me with a good living in farming, doing the work that I loved. He allowed me to stay around long enough to see my children grow into fine citizens and lovers of Christ. A few days ago, he even allowed me to meet my precious baby granddaughter. And he allowed me to share my faith with others.

Rather than feeling sorry for myself for what I might miss out on in the years ahead in this life, I instead give thanks for all that I have had while I was here. In addition to my family, I give thanks for the many friends I have made along the way in the community, in church, and among the young people with whom I was able to share some of my life's experiences. I consider it a true blessing to have known all of you. I thank God for allowing me to live the American Dream. It's hard for me to imagine a better life than what I have had.

Dennis took a deep breath, paused for a moment, and then continued:

For those of you who have a personal relationship with our Lord and savior, you understand why I did not fear death. While I've had a wonderful life here on earth and I will miss all of you, I know that I will have an even better life in the presence of my Lord for eternity.

> For those of you who have not yet given your life to the Lord, I urge you to seek out someone to lead you to him. It is by the grace of God that I have lived such a fulfilling life. I want the same for all of you. Trust in the Lord with all your heart.

Only sniffles could be heard over the blanket of silence in the worship center as Dennis left the podium stand and Pastor David made his way back to the altar.

The pastor invited everyone to join in on one final hymn. He then gave instructions on the dismissal and invited everyone to the cemetery for the graveside service.

Following the service, Jordan gathered the team together on the parking lot and asked for a show of hands for those who wanted to attend the graveside service. The vote appeared to be a unanimous *yes*.

The local police had been notified of the anticipated long funeral procession, and with the help of the Fire police, they had the side streets blocked. As the hearse passed by each officer, they stood at attention and held a salute until the family vehicles had passed through. At the tail end of the procession were the two charter buses carrying the Maryland Terrapins football team.

Trace and the rest of the family couldn't believe their eyes when they saw the team lining up around the grave site.

Pastor David read Scripture verses and offered a final prayer for Pete and comfort for the family. He then concluded, "May we all be comforted in knowing that at some point in the past few days, the gates of heaven were opened for Peter Myers. One can envision Pete standing before the Lord as he gazes into Pete's eyes and, with a pleasing smile, says, 'Well done, my good and faithful servant. Great is your reward.'"

As the pastor moved forward to console the seated family, suddenly, the sound of a bagpipe was heard in the still air. Everyone turned to see Marine Gunnery Sergeant Tom McNickle in his full dress blue uniform, playing "Amazing Grace." Undetected by anyone during the service, Gunny McNickle had perched himself on top of a knoll about thirty-five yards from the gathering.

Dennis could not hold back the tears. He couldn't believe his buddy would do this for him.

The crowd stood in silence as the bagpiper finished the second verse. He then did a perfect about-face and began the next verse as he slowly marched away and disappeared over the backside of the knoll.

A solemn Pastor David turned back to the gathering and proclaimed, "What a fitting farewell for an incredible man."

Slowly, the crowd began to disperse. The football team boarded the buses and headed back to College Park. Jordan observed that many of his teammates were visibly touched by what they had witnessed.

CHAPTER 16

Decision Time for Jordan

The day after the funeral, Trace called Coach Frye to thank him for organizing the team to attend the services. Trace said he had received many comments and messages from those in attendance about what a moving experience it was to see all those young men come through the line to express their condolences.

The coach acknowledged Trace's gratitude, then added, "As their coach, it gave me a great deal of pride to see them there." He continued, "Son, what you saw yesterday was an expression of support for a player who has earned the respect of his teammates. They did not come there because you are a great quarterback who led them to a title. They came because of the person you are and the example you set for them."

The coach added, "When Jordan got the word about your dad's passing, he shared your story with some other team members. He explained the *real reason* why you came to Maryland. I don't believe many of our players can fully comprehend that kind of love and family loyalty. In fact, I myself struggle to relate to that. When he asked if any of them would be interested in attending your dad's service, he was pleased to see that most of them said yes. Some of your teammates were unable to attend due to class schedules and final exams. But those that could wanted to be there for you. The university agreed to pay for the buses."

Trace humbly replied, "Thank you, Coach."

Trace then called Jordan to express his appreciation for bringing the team to Frederick to support him and his family. "You have no idea how much that meant to me," he proclaimed.

Jordan replied, "Brother, I know it meant a lot to you. It also meant a lot to me and the team. I wish you could have seen the reaction of those guys during the service and especially when Dennis read your father's message. Then at the cemetery, when that bagpiper appeared, I turned to see this group of big, tough, macho football players with tears running down their cheeks. What I'm trying to say is, I believe the events of yesterday will stick with them the rest of their lives and may very well serve as a significant step to bringing many of them to a closer relationship with the Lord. It was, indeed, an extraordinary day."

Jordan then added, "By the way, do you think we can get together for lunch one day next week? I have something I need to talk to you about for which I need your advice."

Trace replied, "Sure, how about next Tuesday at the diner. Say eleven forty-five?"

"Works for me. See you there," Jordan confirmed.

The following Tuesday, they met as scheduled. After placing their order, Jordan began to speak. "I just learned last week that I can apply for another year of eligibility for football. Since I only played in four full games during my junior year due to the injury, I can apply for an exemption and play for another year."

As he was speaking, Trace's eyes lit up and his smile got wider. He then exclaimed, "Wow! That's great news. Does the coach know about this?"

Jordan replied, "Not yet. I don't think he ever considered the possibility. He knows that I graduate next week. What he doesn't know is that I have enrolled in some postgraduate studies for the fall semester. I plan to be on campus for at least another year."

"Okay, so you said you wanted my advice?" Trace said. "Well, here it is. You need to let the coach know about this right away. I'm sure he would be blown away to learn of this. I'm not sure what his recruiting class looks like, but you are a proven running back, who brings much more flexibility to our offense. I'm starting to feel vibes for another run at the title."

Jordan laughed. "I agree. If everyone stays healthy, we are going to be hard to beat. I'll set up a meeting with the coach to discuss this. Oh, there is one other thing. My mother would like for you to accompany her and Janis for my graduation next Friday."

Trace was shocked. "Are you kidding me? I would be honored to do that! Give me her number, and I'll call her to set up a time to meet, or if she wishes, I can pick them up at your house."

The following day, Jordan went to see Coach Frye and expressed his desire to return to the team for another season. The coach's jaw literally dropped as he pondered another season of a Myers-Pearce backfield.

"By all means," Coach exclaimed, "I'll get the paperwork filled out, and we will apply for the NCAA exemption. You just made my day."

CHAPTER 17

The Coach's Conversion

On Tuesday, July 1, Trace received a call from Coach Frye.

After exchanging hellos, the coach said, "I want to invite you to join my wife and I at our church at nine in the morning on Sunday, July 13. I really would like for you to be there. I have already spoken to Jordan, and he has accepted the invitation."

Trace replied, "Ah, okay. I'm sure I can be there, but what's this all about? Do I need to prepare any kind of speech or message?"

"No, son," Coach answered, "I just need for you to be present. It means a lot to me."

After confirming and saying goodbye to the coach, Trace immediately called Jordan.

"Hey, buddy," said Trace, "what's going on with the coach? He wants both of us to be there at his church on the thirteenth. Do you know what's happening?"

Jordan answered, "I have no idea. I just know that he made it sound like it was important to him. I gotta tell you, I've been around Coach Frye for four years now, and I don't recall him ever speaking about his church or his relationship with God. All I know is the coach wants us there, and I told him to count on me."

"I told him the same," said Trace. "He gave me the address. I will meet you in front of the church."

On Sunday, July 13, Trace and Jordan, both dressed in suits and ties, arrived at the church in Silver Spring, Maryland, not far from

College Park. It was a diverse evangelical church with what appeared to be several hundred attendees. A number of the parishioners recognized the football players and welcomed them. Coach Frye greeted them in the vestibule and escorted them to the front row of seats were his wife, Barb, was already seated. The two athletes still had no idea why they were there.

The worship team performed both contemporary Christian music and traditional hymns. With the completion of the last song, Pastor Matthew came forward and offered the opening prayer.

Then the middle-aged Pastor addressed the congregation. "Last week, I announced that we would have some guest speakers for today's service. At their request, I purposely did not give you their names. You will soon learn why."

The pastor continued, "To set the stage for this, I will tell you the sequence of events that led to this day. This past February, I received a phone call from a gentleman, who said he was in his mid-fifties. The gentleman went on to explain that he had not been brought up in a worshipping, church-going family. As a result, he did not have a relationship with God. He went on to explain to me that, over the past two years, he had the pleasure of working with two young men who had a steadfast walk with the Lord. He observed their lives, how they handled themselves, how they treated others, and how they always seemed to be in control of their lives. After observing these two young men, he realized what he had missed out on when he was growing up. He then said to me, 'My question to you, pastor, is, can you help me learn what it's like to walk with the Lord?'"

Trace and Jordan looked at each other with a puzzled expression as if to say, *Can this be our coach?*

The pastor went on to say, "When I heard this gentleman's request, I was ecstatic. After saying a silent hallelujah, I replied, "Sir, that's my job. It is my labor of love. I would be honored to serve as your teacher and lead you into a relationship with our Lord and savior.""

Pastor continued, "We then agreed to meet here at the church for two hours every Tuesday evening for the next six to eight weeks to take the journey to salvation. The gentleman on the phone then asked, 'Would it be all right if my wife joined me? She would also like to give her life to the Lord.' After another silent hallelujah, I replied, 'By all means.'"

The pastor then proudly announced, "This couple is here with us today as fully devoted followers of Christ. They would like to share with you their testimony and how important it is to be a godly example for others. Please welcome the coach of the national champion Maryland Terrapins football team, Coach Ronald Frye and his wife, Barbara."

There was applause, and some people were actually standing as the couple approached the platform in the front of the church. Ron and Barb acknowledged them and smiled.

Trace and Jordan looked at each other in disbelief. Now they knew why the coach wanted them there today.

Coach Frye then spoke. "Thank you, Pastor, for that introduction. Ladies and gentlemen, I did not come here today as a football coach. Instead, we stand before you as new Christians, proud to have recently been adopted into the family of God. At this time, I would like to turn the mike over to my wife. She is far more eloquent than I am."

Barb stepped forward and began, "What a joy it is to be here today to share our story. Ron and I have been married for more than thirty years. We have three grown daughters and two grandchildren. My father and mother were raised as Catholics. However, they were not strict practicing Catholics. My brother, sister, and I went to public schools, and we seldom attended Mass."

Barb continued, "For as long as I have known Ron, he has always been involved in football. After his college-playing days were over, he served as a graduate assistant, an offensive coordinator, an assistant coach, and, now, here at Maryland, as a head coach. Knowing the passion he had for the game, I always supported him and accepted any of his shortcomings as a husband and father. Most of the conversations around our house were centered around football. It was hard to get him to discuss or focus on anything but football, especially from August through December."

The coach's wife went on to say, "Last fall, long before the national championship, I noticed a change in him. Even with the season in full swing, he would come home and ask about the family, how my day was. 'Let's go out to dinner, how about a Sunday drive?' After about a month of this, I couldn't take it anymore, so I finally asked the tough guy coach what had changed that suddenly football did not consume every waking moment of the day? I will now let the coach give you his answer."

The coach came forward to speak. "Barb is right, like she usually is. My whole life was centered around football. It was the one thing that I always felt comfortable with. For me, it was a lot easier than being a husband or father. Shame on me! Obviously, God knew I needed help with my priorities, so he used football to send two people into my life that made me stand up and take notice of the misguided path I had been following."

Trace and Jordan glanced at each other, wondering what was next.

The coach continued, "Over the past two years, I have watched two young men from entirely different backgrounds set a godly example for anyone who knew them. I watched as a team of young men showed their respect for them. I watched as several of the players went to them for advice. I watched as they always kept their emotions in check. I watched them lead by example, not just on the field but in their personal lives also. I marveled at how such young people could maintain such discipline. I also watched them as they led their teammates onto the field to openly pray for a fallen athlete. After observing this over the past two seasons, I realized that I might be the coach but these guys are the teachers and the *real* leaders of my team. So when Barb asked what had changed me, I simply explained what I had witnessed on my team. Then I told her, 'I want what they have.'"

"Before I go any further," Coach said, "I asked these two young men to be here today to hear this. I'm sure these humble men are surprised by what they have heard. But they are the reason that Barb and I are standing before you today. One comes from the inner city of Baltimore. The other comes from a farm in Frederick County. Really not much in common, except football and their love for the

Lord. Somehow, God brought them to my team, and they became best friends. Ladies and gentlemen, I want you to meet Jordan Pearce and Trace Myers."

The congregation applauded as Jordan and Trace stood and turned to face them with waving hands and thumbs-up. They then sat down.

Chocking back the tears, the coach continued, "We should all learn a lesson from these two young men. Through their example, they have led others to a deeper relationship with God. They allowed the light of the Lord to shine through their lives. And we should all do the same. Thank you, and God bless all of you."

Pastor Matthew returned to the pulpit and gave a brief message from John chapter 5 about the importance of letting others see Jesus in your life. He then offered the closing prayer. Appropriately, the worship team closed the service by performing the hymn, "Let Others See Jesus in You."

After the service, many parishioners came forward to hug Ron and Barb. Trace and Jordan received many compliments for their living testimonies and their performance on the football field.

It was truly a wonderful day.

CHAPTER 18

The 2008 Season

Jordan Pearce was able to get the exemption from the NCAA and was eligible to play his final season as a graduate student. The news of his return spread quickly.

On the first day of preseason practice, Coach Frye held his customary morning team meeting.

In the front of the room, he had on display last year's national championship trophy. He then did his usual welcome and introductions. As the meeting came to a close, the coach asked that everyone join him as he offered a word of prayer for the team.

The room got quiet as everyone bowed their heads. The coach began.

"Dear Father in heaven, we come before you today to ask for your blessing on this band of brothers. Keep us strong and healthy as we prepare for this season. No matter what our win and loss record is, we ask that you spare us from any serious injury. More important than our record, let us maintain the reputation we have for sportsmanship. Let us not forget to live up to that standard. Finally, Father, I ask that you watch over each and every one of these young men. Lead them, guide them, and protect them from the evils that exist in this world. Let them see their needs to walk with you, to have you in their hearts, and to accept you as their savior and salvation. We pray this in the name of Jesus. Amen!"

Trace and Jordan raised their heads and looked at each other in amazement. They then looked at the coach and realized that he did not read that prayer from notes. It was truly from his heart.

The Maryland Terrapins began the season, ranking third in the AP Poll. They picked up from where they left off last year, winning their first ten games decisively. In week eleven, they lost a heartbreaking, hard-fought battle to Florida State on a last-minute field goal.

Maryland finished the season with an 11–1 record and was again ranked second in the AP Poll, entitling them to another trip to the BCS college football championship to face the Oklahoma Sooners in Miami Gardens, Florida, on January 8.

On December 14, the Heisman Trophy was awarded to Maryland quarterback, Trace Myers.

In the BCS championship game, the Maryland Terrapins executed their game plan to near perfection on both sides of the ball. They beat the Oklahoma Sooners by a score of 35–14 for their second consecutive national title.

CHAPTER 19

The Off-Season

In mid-January, following the championship, Jordan contacted Trace and invited him to dinner at a nice restaurant. When Trace arrived, he was surprised to see Jordan's girlfriend, Marla, there with him.

Trace joked, "Now I know why we are at a nice restaurant. You wouldn't dare take her to the diner that we usually go to."

Jordan smiled and came back at Trace. "That's right, buddy, and I would never invite you here if it wasn't for her."

After ordering dinner, Jordan spoke, "As you know, Marla and I have been dating for more than a year and a half. What you don't know is that this past Christmas, I asked her to marry me. She accepted, and we plan to marry in June. My question to you is, since you are my best friend, would you be my best man?"

Trace answered with a beaming smile, "I would be honored to be your best man. I am so happy for both of you."

Jordan added, "I have some other good news, which kind of helped in our decision to get married. The firm that I interned for last summer has offered me an engineering position."

Trace declared, "Wow! So you win a national title in January, you're getting married to this beautiful lady in June, and you're starting your career in the field which you longed for! Is God good or what?"

Trace offered the blessing. They enjoyed their meal and then went on their way.

During the first week of February, Coach Frye contacted Trace and requested a meeting for the two of them. Trace suspected that the coach had accepted a head coaching job at another university. The rumors had been floating around about a number of schools contacting him.

When Trace arrived for the meeting, after hellos, he said, "Okay, Coach, I know why I'm here. Where are you coaching next year?"

Coach Frye smiled and shook his head and said jokingly, "You know, son, you really think you know it all, don't you?

Trace responded, "Come on, Coach, you've just won two consecutive national championships. Are you telling me you haven't been offered more money to go elsewhere?"

The coach sat back in his desk chair and said, "That's not why I called you here. But since you seem to know so much, let me set the record straight as to my plans for the future. I still have two years left on my contract. I intend to honor that contract and then retire. I will then be sixty years old, and as you know, there now are more important things in my life than football. Yes, I have been contacted by other colleges, but I have not accepted any invitations to interview. I am not so naïve to believe that I'm a great coach. We won those national titles because we had a special chemistry on this team, thanks to you and Jordan. We also had one of the best quarterbacks I have ever watched play. In other words, I was blessed, I know it, and I'm staying right here until retirement. That's my future. Now let's talk about yours, which is the real reason why I called you here."

Trace said with an approving smile, "I am so glad to hear that you're staying. I'm also glad to hear that you have your priorities in order. It has been a joy to watch God work in your life. So what do you want to know about my future?"

"Here are the facts," said the coach, "I am not only getting calls from other universities, I am also getting calls from NFL teams, wanting to know if you plan to enter the draft in April. I don't know what to tell them because you have never said anything about your intentions. I'm certainly not going to advise you on this, but the truth is, you have two national titles and a Heisman Trophy, you've set nearly every school record for a QB. What is there left for you to achieve at the college level? You would definitely get drafted in the first round and probably be the number one pick. There's a lot of money out there for you, Trace."

Trace responded, "Well, Coach, to be honest with you, I haven't given it much thought. I still need twelve credits to get my degree. I am aware of the money that's out there, but as you know, that's not what motivates me. I came here to get my degree. The money will still be there after I graduate. I realize we are losing a lot of key players this year, but I still think we can have a successful season."

The coach then asked, "But, Trace, what if you got injured in your senior year? Do you really want to risk your football future?"

Trace then smiled and said, "Coach, you know me well enough by now. If that would happen, I would accept it as part of God's plan and go on with my life. I'm staying here for this season."

The coach, smiling and shaking his head, replied. "I'm not sure that, if I were in your shoes, I would be making the same decision. But who am I to question your judgment? For me, this is good news. I look forward to another year of having you around. I'll let the AD know so he can get out a news release. Perhaps then, the calls will stop coming."

On Saturday, June 28, Jordan and Marla were married. It was a simple wedding at the church where Marla attended since she was a little girl. Jordan's mother, grandmother, and his twin sisters were all dressed in matching outfits. Following the ceremony, they gathered for the reception. Rather than the best man proposing a toast to the bride and groom, Trace decided to offer a prayer. After the meal, the music started. Trace took Jaedyn's hand and asked her to dance. Everyone in the room was touched as they watched the six-foot-five-inch gentle giant dance with the autistic twenty-year-old girl. The proud Jaedyn could not get the smile off her face.

CHAPTER 20

The 2009 Season

The Terrapins entered the season with only nine returning starters from last year's championship team. No members of last year's offensive line returned. As a result, they had a preseason ranking of number 23 in the AP Poll. The season got off to a rough start as they lost to number 12 California at Berkley 35–13. Trace struggled to create any offensive attack as he was constantly under pressure. They also struggled to get the running game going.

In week number 2, they barely beat James Madison (JMU) in overtime in a home game at Byrd Stadium.

On September 19, they faced Middle Tennessee State at home. The Blue Raiders were unranked but were known for their formidable pass rush. The young inexperienced Maryland offensive line could not contain them. Trace was under pressure with every snap.

Midway into the second quarter, Trace dropped back to pass. He managed to get the pass off as he was being pushed back by two defensive linemen. He fell backward and landed with his upper back on the helmet of another attacking Blue Raider. The big QB was in great pain.

A hush fell over the forty-three thousand fans at Byrd Stadium as Trace was attended to by the medical team. As expected, Trace's teammates moved onto the field in unison and kneeled in prayer. Coach Frye stood over his quarterback with much concern. The coach knew this was a serious injury.

The ambulance came onto the field, and Trace was put on a board with a neck brace. As he was being carted to the ambulance, every single Maryland player came to his side to wish him well.

They knew they had lost their leader. Trace gave thumbs-up to his teammates and the crowd before he was rolled into the ambulance. The crowd stood in applause to acknowledge their All-American quarterback as a gesture of their concern for his well-being.

At the hospital, the X-rays and tests showed that Trace had suffered damage to two vertebrae in his upper back and damage to his spinal cord. They were unable to determine the extent of the damage to his spinal cord due the swelling. Brian and Lori arrived at the hospital later that evening.

Many calls came into the hospital, inquiring of his condition. The next morning, Coach Frye and Jordan Pearce showed up to be there when Trace was allowed to have visitors.

After the swelling and inflammation subsided, the medical professionals were able to do more tests. Once the tests were completed, Trace was allowed to have visitors. He was in traction, able to speak but needed to stay still.

At about 1:20 p.m., the attending physician entered the room with the test results. He asked Coach and Jordan to leave the room while he spoke with Trace and his family members. The doctor informed Trace that he had extensive damage to his spinal cord. That, combined with his back injury, was going to require many months of healing and therapy. He told Trace that his football season was over. He added, "I hate to be the bearer of bad news, but depending on how you heal, there's a chance you may never be able to play again."

Trace closed his eyes and took a deep breath. He then thanked the doctor for his honesty.

Brian and Lori came to his side to comfort and encourage him following this sad news.

Trace looked at them, forced a smile, and said, "As Dad would say, 'I guess this is all part of God's plan.'"

The news of Trace's season-ending injury sent shock waves throughout Terrapin Nation and the college football world.

As Trace began to mend physically and mentally, he finally accepted his situation and prayed every day for God to give him the strength he needed to recover. Arrangements were made for him to leave the hospital and go into a nearby rehab facility. Prior to leaving the hospital, his therapist paid him a visit. She was a tall, thin lady in her early twenties. Her name was Cheryl.

After introducing herself, Cheryl asked if he would mind if she prayed for him.

Trace was touched by this and felt certain that Cheryl and he would get along. He then answered her, "By all means."

Cheryl began. "Dear Father in heaven. We come before you today to ask for your guidance and intervention as we begin this long journey for Trace's recovery. Give me the wisdom I need to prepare a program that will help this man regain his strength. Give him the patience he needs to eventually see the results. Father, we know that it is through your guidance and grace we can achieve this mission. We pray this in the name of Jesus our Lord and savior. Amen."

The next day, Trace was moved to the rehab center, and the therapy began. Over the next several weeks, Cheryl worked with Trace for ninety minutes every day, except weekends. With each passing day, the intensity of his pain lessened and his mobility improved slowly but surely.

Much to Trace's dismay, the end of the season saw the inexperienced Terrapins finish with a 2 and 10 record.

CHAPTER 21

Decision Time for Trace

Over time, the bond with his therapist became more than a patient-provider relationship. Cheryl would show up even on weekends. She would visit him after church on Sundays, and they would read Scripture together. She took the time to connect with his instructors and obtained lessons and lecture notes for him so he wouldn't fall behind in his studies. It became very obvious to Trace that this girl was something special. When his mom and family members came to visit, he told them about this remarkable Christian lady that was caring for him.

Trace progressed to the point that he was able to go home for the Christmas holiday. However, he needed to wear a back brace during his waking hours. Cheryl and Trace called each other every day while he was away. After the holiday, he returned to classes for the next semester, wearing the brace. He still required therapy three times a week.

Their feelings for each other grew stronger with each passing week. Their love grew to the point where they started talking about the future.

One evening, Cheryl decided to have a heart-to-heart talk with the man she had fallen in love with. She began, "I know that football means a lot to you and your plans were to play professionally. But as your therapist and someone who cares deeply for you, I think you need to know that, if something like this injury ever happens again, you could be crippled for life. I feel you need to think long and hard about your return to the playing field."

Trace had a concerned look on his face as he asked, "Does this mean that if I choose to play pro football, you wouldn't marry me?"

Cheryl replied, "Trace, I just can't bear the thought of seeing you go through life as an invalid. You have so much going for you other than football. You are an intelligent, godly man with great leadership skills and a bigger-than-life personality. That's why I love you the way you are. I know you can make a lot of money playing pro football, but what good does that do to you if you have to face life as a cripple?"

Trace thought for a moment. Finally, he looked into Cheryl's eyes and said, "This might be the most unusual proposal ever given." He then gazed upward and said, "So I'm faced with the decision of continuing my football career or spending the rest of my life with the woman God sent me of whom I truly love." He then lowered his head and said to Cheryl, "So I guess the only football I will be playing in the future will be in *our* backyard with *our* children."

Cheryl burst into tears and leaped into his arms. Trace got the biggest hug of his life. Cheryl was unable to speak through the sobbing. Finally, Trace loosened the embrace and wiped away some of her tears. He then asked, "Does this mean you will marry me?

Cheryl emphatically responded, "Yes! Yes! Yes!" The two embraced again.

Finally, Cheryl broke the embrace, stood back with her hands on her hips, and said, "That's the most off-the-wall proposal I've ever heard of. That sure wasn't the way that I ever dreamed it would be."

Trace laughed as he asked, "Are you upset with me?"

Cheryl responded with a smile, "Of course not you, big silly. This is the happiest day of my life."

The following weekend, Trace and Cheryl went to the farm for dinner with the family. After dinner, they announced their plans to get married in the fall. The family was very pleased, as they knew how Trace felt about Cheryl.

Trace also informed the family that, given the extent of his injury, he has decided not to continue his football career. Everyone at the table knew how difficult that decision was for Trace, but they all were relieved to hear that.

Trace graduated in May. His mother, Brian and Addie, Lori, Dennis, Cheryl, Jordan, and Coach Frye were in attendance at the ceremony. He was still wearing a brace but was walking normal and without pain.

CHAPTER 22

God's Plan for All

Coach Ronald Frye, as promised, finished out his contract and retired. He and his wife, Barbara, moved to North Carolina to be closer to their grandchildren. As a successful football coach and a devoted follower of Christ, he is often invited as a guest speaker for church groups and service clubs. He and Barb never get tired of telling the story that led them to the Lord.

Jordan Pearce is enjoying a successful career with the state of Maryland as a civil engineer. He and his wife, Marla, now have a boy and a girl. They live in a quiet neighborhood in Baltimore County. He and Trace are still best friends. Jordan was the best man in Trace's wedding. He is an elder in his church and active with the youth group.

Judith Myers still lives in the farmhouse and has poured herself into church work and watching the grandkids. She hosts a weekly women's Bible study. She is very proud of her large vegetable garden and spends much of her time taking care of it.

Brian and Addie Myers continue to farm and manage the overall business. They are still very active with the 4-H. They now have two daughters. They built a new home on the farm to accommodate their growing family. They are expecting their third child.

Dennis Myers decided to make a career of the Marine Corps. After a deployment in Afghanistan, he returned as a gunnery sergeant and now serves under the base commanding officer of Marine Corps Base Quantico in Virginia. He plans to marry within the year,

Lori Myers is serving as assistant director of special education services for Frederick County. She and recently ordained pastor Nathan Holmes are planning a fall wedding.

Trace and Cheryl Myers were married in October, following his graduation. They moved into the small home that Brian and Addie were in. Cheryl continued her career as a physical therapist but transferred to Frederick County. Trace took a job with the University of Maryland Extension service, assisting farmers with record keeping, land and herd management, and taxes. In this capacity with his name recognition, he is also an unofficial ambassador for the University of Maryland. He and Cheryl have an agreement with their employers for extended time off, allowing them to do missionary work in Third World countries. They share a passion for reaching the unreached for the glory of God. They teach crop farming. They assist with building churches, and they spread the gospel.

EPILOGUE

A reflection on what would not have happened had it not been *for the love of Pete.*

Trace Myers would not have attended the University of Maryland.

Trace and Jordan would have never become lifelong best friends.

The lives of many of their teammates would have never been touched in such a positive way by the example set by Trace and Jordan.

The Maryland Terrapins would not have likely won a national championship, let alone two of them.

The University of Maryland may have never received the recognition given to them as a result of the conduct and sportsmanship of their football team.

Pete Myers may never have seen his son play for the national title.

Coach Ronald Frye and his wife, Barbara, may not have ever come to know the Lord, and they would not be working to lead others to a closer relationship with God.

Trace would have never met Cheryl, the love of his life. The two of them would not be serving the Lord together in foreign countries, spreading the gospel.

All of this, as a result of the love for one godly man.

For the love of Pete.

As Pete would say—"It was all part of God's plan."

May the grace of the Lord Jesus Christ,
and the love of God,
and the fellowship of the Holy Spirit
be with you all.

—2 Corinthians 13:14

ABOUT THE AUTHOR

P. Grant Gartrell was the fifth child born into a family of seven children. He spent his youth on a farm in Carroll County, Maryland, before moving to the suburbs of Baltimore at the age of fourteen. Growing up, his family did not attend church regularly.

After graduating from high school, he attended a computer tech school for one year. He then enlisted in the United States Marine Corps. He served in Vietnam in a noncombat role. He received an honorable discharge at the rank of sergeant. He then met his soon-to-be wife, Barbara. Together, they have four grown children and eleven grandchildren.

Most of his career has been in sales. After working four years in the Philadelphia area, he and Barb moved their family to South Central Pennsylvania. It was then they began to attend a Bible-preaching evangelical church. Thanks to the efforts and teachings of a dedicated pastor from that church, he gave his life to the Lord.

Since that day, he has always felt that God had chosen him to do something special to glorify his name. He asked the Lord to show him what it was that he would have him do on his behalf. No doubt, the story contained in this book is one of those assignments from God.